BIG GAME

ALEX LAYBOURNE

SEVERED PRESS
Hobart Tasmania

BIG GAME

'This is for my wife Patty, and our wonderful children. James, Logan, Ashleigh, Damon, and Riley.'

CHAPTER 1

SOMEWHERE? AFRICA
NOVEMBER, 2014

"This is Dr. Julian Grau, recording cross-over attempt number twenty-seven. All previous attempts have yielded negative results, but this time, with an increased polarity on the shift mechanism, we have made progress to a deeper level," Julian spoke into his handheld voice recorder as he paced around the lab.

The large structure that occupied the center of the room was a crazy-looking contraption with eight iron arms that curled upwards from the floor before coming close to meeting at their apex. All eight arms crackled with electricity. Blue flakes jumped the gaps between the eight tips. Some even ran down the arms into the floor, which had been fully rubberized after the seventh experiment.

Julian had lost his entire team on that trial, and had almost lost his funding for the project. He was lucky that his means were not funded by any government or political movement. Well, not directly at least. He was working under the instruction of a large private corporation, and alongside unlimited funds, he had been given an unlimited amount for personal means also; his salary was a blank cheque that he could fill at any time.

"The start-up is holding steady. I am preparing to introduce the alternative energy source and make a connection to whatever lays beyond." Julian couldn't help but shout as he spoke, his enthusiasm getting the better of him.

A few moments later, licks of a vibrant red light began to dance alongside the blue. The red steadily increased until it matched the blue power and eventually overtook it, consuming it.

"Alternative power source is fully in control and holding steady," Julian spoke, his excitement at a peak.

Walking away from the machine, backing up so he did not have to turn away from the wondrous sight, Julian moved to the central console. His hands found the control panel and blindly pushed the buttons he needed to. A slow whine began to build, like the hull doors of a great ship slowly opening for the first time after a long voyage. The ground began to shake, the building they were in to tremble. Alarms began to sound, but none of them were directly connected to the Spider, aptly named based on its final constructed appearance.

"The connection has been established, and the Spider is holding strong. Preparing to punch through the barriers." He needed to shout now for his voice to be heard above the din.

One final dial was adjusted and the Spider began to groan. The eight curled legs moved, closing in on one another until only a few inches separated them. There was a dull heavy thud. It came from within the room, and the force of the blast could be felt like a sudden burst of warm air, which hit like a right hook to the stomach. Yet the noise itself seemed to come from a long distance away, muted.

"We did it. Connection achieved with the other side." Julian gave a triumphant cry. With the connection established, the Spider seemed to steady itself. The groaning and growling subsided.

Julian jumped when the round of applause struck up behind him. He spun to face the rest of his team with a look of pure jubilation etched onto his features.

"I can't believe it. You did it." Tracy van der Meer walked forward and hugged Julian. He responded by taking her into his arms and kissing her deeply.

"Hey, I know it's a breakthrough, but I hope you don't congratulate me like that," Luc de Waal answered. He stepped up to the pair and clapped Julian on the back before offering him a firm handshake.

"Well, I figured now was a good time to bring us out into the public." Julian slid his arm around Tracy and held her tight.

"I'm happy for you." Luc smiled, the blooming romance overpowering the historic impact of the moment. He knew everything Julian had gone through. They had been friends since they were children.

"So, what do we do now?" Tracy asked bringing the group back to the task at hand. "We have just broken through the barriers of time. That's pretty big." A silence fell as the size of the moment washed over them.

The electric currents that ran through the curled arms of the Spider were condensed into a solid beam that ran through each limb, climbing from the base to the curled tips. Converging at that point the beam then fell to form a floating orb of red light which was steadily expanding. The shape stretching vertically to fill the space beneath the Spider's legs.

Julian moved away from the group to check the readouts on the various dials and monitors. "The connection is strong and stable. We have anchored on the other side. I could never have imagined we would achieve this." There was a bounce to Julian's words that made him sound like a child staring at gifts on Christmas morning.

"Do you know what this means? This is a breakthrough. A real scientific breakthrough." Tracy was equally as excited. "We need to tell people. Announce this to the world. I mean, this opens up the possibility of ..."

"We will not be telling anybody anything, Miss van der Meer," a voice from the shadows cut her off.

The trio turned around in shock. They had been working on the Spider for almost eight months, and not once had they ever had so much as a phone call let alone a guest. Their research lab was not only stationed in the middle of the Free State territory, but they were located deep beneath the surface, locked away from the world.

"Who's there?" Luc called out. An ex-marine in what was now called the Maritime Reaction Squad, he was not known for his calm approach when dealing with things. In his years, he had done a great many things, a number of those he was not proud of, and would never talk about, but he was a man willing to take any measures to ensure the safety of this team and their mission.

Luc had been hired by Julian specifically for the Spider program, and had been more than happy to take the offer of a permanent pay cheque. He was even more delighted when he saw the amount it would be for every month.

"Easy there, Mr. de Waal. You may be a tough man, but I am a powerful one. A false move and everything you know about the world will come crashing down around you." The voice was calm and cool, spoken without a trace of emotion. It caught Luc off guard. He was not used to being spoken to in such a way.

"Show yourself," he growled.

Julian moved behind his friend and placed a hand on his shoulder. He felt his friend's body stiffen with rage. "It's alright, Luc. I believe we have the honour of meeting our primary benefactor." Julian recognized the voice from his previous dealings with the man. All of which had been telephonic.

Slowly, a figure emerged from the shadows. At first, the presence escaped notice, for everybody was waiting for someone much taller to appear. The owner of the voice rolled into view, his electric wheelchair moving silently into position before the Spider.

"It is magnificent. A job well done, Dr. Grau." The man was in genuine awe of the structure. "I knew I had made the right decision when I chose you." He turned his head and smiled, the chair following to bring him face to face with the group. The man's face was stern, his features sharp and his eyes as cold as steel. The bridge of his nose was so defined it gave the impression that you would cut yourself the moment you touched it.

That the man had money was not in question, the air of high breeding seeped from him like a cheap cologne, and with it came an air of danger. Not of a thrill seeker, or of a man whose adventurous life was responsible for this physical situation, but the sort of danger that comes from a man who had no conscience, no remorse. It was the sort of danger that came from a man of bad intentions.

"Allow me to introduce myself." He spoke politely, with a voice that hid his accent well. It was impossible to guess where he was from, an intentional trait worked into his voice through years of practice. The man had created himself to be invisible until he chose otherwise, which only served to add to his persona. "My name is Albert Wilhelm III. I do not expect that you have heard of me, yet I can assure you, I know everything there is to know about you. Including you, Mr. de Waal. That job you did in Witbank, for example." Albert smiled as he watched the colour drain from Luc's face.

"How did you …" Luc stammered, caught off guard and made to feel uncomfortable. Nobody knew his past, where he had been, what he had done, and there was a reason for it.

"It is one of my jobs to know things. Especially about the employees working on a job like this for me. Don't worry, as long as we remain on good-working terms, your secrets will be safe." There was a glimmer in the man's eyes that told a different story, but none of them were willing to mention it.

"Excuse me, but if you don't want the media here, why did we build this thing?" Tracy asked, stepping half a step ahead of Julian. Far enough to be seen as standing on her own, but close enough to still feel the comfort of his shadow connecting with hers. "This could revolutionise the world. Who knows what we have connected to, and this is just the start …" Tracy began to talk faster and faster as the words formed in her mind seconds before being thrown into the conversation. It was her natural way, but Albert was not having any of it.

"On the contrary, Miss van der Meer, I know exactly where that portal is linked to. When we started this project, I was very specific in the range and frequencies I gave you all. I would hope that you have not deviated from those numbers." Albert made no attempt to hide the venom in his words.

"No, not at all, sir," Julian answered nervously.

"Good," Albert sneered. "Then everything is in place. Fear not, we will get our coverage, and you three will receive all of the credit, but not yet. The job is only half way done."

"I don't understand …" Tracy began.

"I gave you an unlimited budget, and unlimited wages for a reason. So you don't have to think about things anymore. I was specific because the portal is not the end game, it is merely the conduit. All will become clear in due course." He paused, studying their faces. Albert waited patiently, letting the tension grow before speaking once more. "I think it is time to run the first real penetration test. Don't you?"

The three friends were speechless. Behind them, the Spider was holding steady. The red orb of energy had grown to the point that it was almost as tall as the space it was given. Julian cast intermittent glances towards the computer consoles. He was nervous. They were playing with something which, if allowed to get out of control, could potentially detonate with enough power to wipe out the entire Free State, not to mention the pollution that would spread across a large part of South Africa. Everything looked good. There were no bells ringing, or sirens blaring, and while earlier attempts at the structure had proven to be unstable in terms of the basic construct, the machine was now holding steady. Yet all of that did little to calm Julian's nerves.

"What do you mean by penetration test?" Julian asked, his voice distant, as if he had just been roused from a dream and was unsure if the conversation was set in reality or the dream world.

"He means he wants to send somebody through," Luc answered, his deep voice and strong accent conveyed the right level of severity and disbelief. Luc stared at the man in the chair. His eyes shone like search lamps against the contrast of his skin which was as dark as pitch. His large square jaw was clenched, his muscular body coiled and ready.

"Very good, Mr. de Waal, very good." Albert smiled. "I already have a candidate waiting." Albert raised his hand and gave a subtle wave of his fingers. Two more men entered the large underground lab. They were flanking a smaller, sickly looking man. The two bodyguards were giants, equal in size and mass to Luc, but even by regular standards, the man they were escorting was tiny.

"I don't know what you are doing, but I will not allow it. I did not sign on for this," Julian thundered. Standing tall, he stared daggers at his rich benefactor.

"If you won't, Dr. Grau, then somebody else will." There were no more words needed. The threat was clear.

"Besides, Mr. Winslow here was more than happy to oblige. You see, his whole family is sick. A disease he brought up from the mines has spread to his wife and children. Now they are all at home dying. There is a drug that can cure them in all but the most advanced cases, but sadly, these things cost money. Isn't that right, Mr. Winslow?" Albert asked the frail-looking man who had been positioned before him.

The man nodded, unable to even muster up the strength to voice his opinion. He trembled violently. His clothes were peppered with blood stains from the coughed-up bloody lumps of congealed lung tissue. There was an odour about him that reeked of death.

"It just happens that my pharmaceutical company is the very one that makes the drug which could save Mr. Winslow and his family, and so we struck a deal. It is a simple arrangement. He will move through the portal, and return instantly. In exchange for this, I will give him the drugs he so desperately seeks."

Beside him, Julian felt Tracy tense and then begin to shake. He put his arm around her waist and pulled her against him.

"We have only just established a stable connection. We cannot send a human subject yet," Tracy began, but a squeeze from Julian and a glare from Albert silenced her. More the latter than the former.

"I am glad we are on the same page, Dr. Grau." Albert stared at Julian. He had seen the gesture to stop Tracy, and foolishly mistook it for loyalty.

A few moments later, the group were back at their stations. Julian monitoring the output from the sensors, Tracy, a computer programmer by trade, was monitoring the systems that Julian used, making sure that everything stayed in sync. Luc was standing between the two of them and their guests. He was staring at the two white men that now flanked Albert's wheelchair. There was something about them he did not trust.

Mr. Winslow had been stripped to his underwear, a sight Tracy in particular would have gladly gone without experiencing. His body covered in sensors and pads that were designed to do everything from monitor his heart rate to record the conditions of the world he was travelling to. He had been re-dressed in a plain jumpsuit provided by one of the men who had escorted him into the building. Standing before the large Spider, he looked smaller than ever. The convict costume he had been placed in was nothing more than a final act of humiliation. The work of a man so power hungry he was blind to the plight of those around him; de-sensitized to the extreme.

"Please tell me we are ready, Dr. Grau. I am growing awfully tired of waiting around," Albert sneered, impatiently.

Julian worked furiously, checking and double checking all of the readings that he had just finished triple checking. He was stalling for time, and he knew it. He had no idea what lay beyond the Spider's portal. He had used the figures and coordinates provided, but that said nothing, for they bore no resemblance to anything physical.

"How would I know?" Julian growled. "The numbers are all holding steady and nothing untoward seems to be happening, but this is new ground."

"I will take that as a yes," Albert answered with cold glee. "Mr. Winslow, if you would be so kind. Remember now, your family is waiting for you." Julian expected the man to start laughing, but he didn't. Albert merely stared at his victim, the man he referred to as Mr. Winslow, allowing the silence to push him on.

Tentatively, through the weariness of his body as much as it was the result of his own trepidations, Mr. Winslow mounted the steps that led to the Spider's central platform. His hair, what thin strands were remaining, began to rise as he got closer to the power core.

"That's right, Mr. Winslow. Just step through, tell us what you see, and then you can come home," Albert coaxed.

Mr. Winslow reached out and poked the red energy core. His fingers found a strange cold. A nothingness that felt soft and warm. His fingers disappeared, and then his hand. He felt something. It was hot, the kind of heat that one experienced getting into a sealed car in the heat of summer, or visiting Florida. He withdrew his hand. It was covered in sweat.

"What is it, Mr. Winslow? My patience only knows certain bounds," Albert prodded, overeager to see his guinea pig cross the threshold.

"It's hot through there. Wherever it is," he spoke softly, his voice tired. It was the voice of a man who had reached the end of the road and already taken a few strides over the cliff face it had led him to, only he had yet to truly notice he was falling.

Mr. Winslow took a deep breath and stepped through. His body vanished without as much as a ripple of disturbance in the surface of the energy core. It was as if he was rubbed out of existence; there one minute and stripped away one inch at a time the next.

"Good Lord, he did it," one of the bodyguards spoke, clearly impressed by the fortitude of a desperate man. Luc gave a *tsk* of disapproval, and turned his back on them.

"Vitals are holding steady. The air temperature is over a hundred degrees, and the humidity is ninety-eight percent." Julian ran through the dials, reading them aloud not to keep Albert informed but through the sheer adrenaline rush of accomplishment.

Then the first alarm sounded. "I've got an accelerated heart rate," Tracy cried out. "Ninety beats a minute, one hundred beats, one-thirty." The readings changed so fast she was not able to enunciate them all quick enough.

"What's happening?" Luc moved towards his colleagues, who stood huddled together pressing frantically at the controls.

"We are losing stability," Tracy called just as the scream rang out.

There was no doubt as to where the cry originated from. It rang out through the gateway unhindered and undistorted, despite the unknown distance and time between them. A hand shot through the barrier, the fingers stretched wide. They were covered in blood, dripping from the digits in thick clotting globs. There was a wet crunch and the scream fell silent. The arm jerked twice, once in each horizontal direction, and with a flat pop, the body burst. At least that was the only logical explanation for the sound, which was similar to the one a cherry tomato makes when being bitten. Blood burst through the portal, splattering the floor and the Spider's base. A foul odour pervaded the room, it was the smell of rot, of disease-riddled offal meeting the humid air of wherever it was that the poor man had been sent.

"Shut it down. Shut it down now," Albert cried, jumping forward in his chair. "Do it, for Christ's sake." There was an urgency in his voice that came close to sounding like fear.

Julian worked furiously powering down the Spider, but it was not fast enough for Albert's liking.

"You fool of a man, shut it down," he roared, fear an unmistakable component of his voice.

"I need to keep it stabilized otherwise we will get blown up along with half this state," Julian barked, but managed to retain his composure. "There, the Spider is offline." He turned around as he spoke, sweat pouring from his forehead. His hair was stuck to his scalp. He felt as if he had just run a marathon.

On the floor, the hand still quivered. It flapped around like a fish. It was short lived, however, for something appeared through the rapidly fading energy core and grabbed up the severed limb, swallowing it whole and disappearing just as the power died completely.

"That was a ..." Julian stammered in disbelief.

"What the hell did you have us do?" Luc roared, striding forward. The two bodyguards moved into position before Albert, and caught Luc mid-advance.

"Easy now, Mr. de Waal, you three just became incredibly wealthy." Albert smiled, and something twinkled in his eyes.

"What are you talking about?" Luc snarled, but there was something in him that was interested. His wild side, the same part that had led him to do the things he had done. It was a simple question, but in that moment, Albert knew that he had them.

"Now is not the time. There is much work to be done. But tonight you will celebrate, and tomorrow, the work starts again." Albert turned his wheelchair around and drove it away. His bodyguards remained where they were. Not moving until they were given the order.

"What about his family?" Tracy called after him. "You said you would help his family." Her voice was strained, tears building behind her eyes.

Albert stopped his exit and turned to face them, his expensive wheelchair rotated on the spot. "Yes, well. The deal was he would come back and I would give him the medication. He didn't come back." He flashed another smile, a snake-like smirk, and was gone. Only once he had left the room did his bodyguards make their own retreat.

"Just try it," one growled at Luc, who stood eyeballing them, his face a picture of intensity.

Slowly, the men backed away and left the lab, leaving the three colleagues to pick up the pieces. The day was supposed to have been their crowning glory, a scientific breakthrough.

"You guys all saw that, right?" Tracy asked once they knew they were alone.

"Oh yeah," Luc answered. "We work for an asshole."

"I meant that thing in the Spider," Tracy corrected him.

"Oh that, right. Yeah, I saw that, too." Luc lowered his voice when answering. He felt dirty, they had sent another man to his death. It seemed his fate to never escape killing.

"So what do we do now?" Julian asked looking at Luc. "Help me out here, old friend."

Luc sighed. "I have worked for people worse than him, but they are all the same. We are stuck until he lets us go. He means it about the money. He has an end game, and we have a role to play, just you wait." Luc reached out and patted the nearest Spider leg as he spoke.

A silence fell over them. They did not know what to say. They were jubilant and deflated in equal measure.

"I need a drink." Julian broke the silence.

"Me, too. We've earned it," Luc agreed. "It's a shame that we don't have anything harder than coffee in this bloody place."

The two old friends moved away from the powerless consoles, resigned to their fate. Tracy remained behind, still lost in thought. Her mind playing catch up with everything she had seen and heard.

"Hey, guys," Tracy called after them, "shouldn't we at least clean up all this blood?"

CHAPTER 2

GHOST TRAIL - NICOLET NATIONAL FOREST
1992

Wallace Carmichael stared at the creature through his binoculars. The deer was a magnificent specimen and would have made an excellent trophy to mark the end of his annual father-son hunting excursion. For five days every summer, he and his two boys, Levi and Matt, would pack up their camping gear and head into the Nicolet National Forest, a three-hour drive from their home.

They spent their days hiking, fishing, and hunting. Wallace loved the outdoors and had been keen to instill the thrill of the hunt into his children. If he had ever had a daughter then she, too, would have become a hunter. He would have seen to it. As luck would have it, he had only sons.

His eldest was a keen hunter and a great shot. Levi was a strapping nineteen-year-old cadet in the local police academy. At over six feet tall, with naturally broad shoulders, he was the apple of his father's eye. When Levi had said he was applying to join the force, it was the proudest day of Wallace's life. His son following in his footsteps. It was his youngest son, who at thirteen was standing on the fringes of his father's patience and understanding. A competent outdoorsman, Matt had declared himself a vegetarian at the age of eleven, much to Wallace's chagrin, and had as of that moment not yet taken a single shot with a rifle, at least not with the intention of making a kill. He was a great shot, even better than his brother, but shied away from the manly world his father had been raised in, and the same world he insisted on raising his children in.

The exasperations had reached a head during their trip, when Matt had taken a book and sat reading while his father and brother went hunting. It was not the book Wallace was annoyed by, for he encouraged his children to pursue their education to the very limits of their abilities, and he could not deny that his youngest was smarter than both he and Levi combined. It was not the book, but the attitude and the timing of it that had angered him.

"Take your time now, Matt. Watch the beast, and when you are ready, take the shot," he coached as his son lay prone, the rifle butt nestled into his shoulder. His heart swelled with pride at the sight, and in his mind he could already see it. He could hear the crack of the rifle and the sound of the beast as it fell to the floor. It was a beautiful white tail that would make not only a fine eating, but also the perfect first kill for his son. His heart swelled with pride, only nothing came. "Don't take too long, Matt, you will lose him," Wallace growled, keeping his voice as low as possible.

"I can't, Dad," the young boy whimpered. "I can't shoot it, please don't make me." He started to cry.

"Jesus Christ, Matt. Take the god damned shot and show me you're a man," Wallace snapped, his patience not wearing out but ending. "Take it now," he roared, startling his son, not to mention the deer, whose head snapped around, alert to the hidden danger.

"No … please don't make me," Matt begged, his body shaking as the tears streamed down his face."

"You are my son, and you will shoot that god damned …" Wallace stopped, his booming voice fell still as he watched the deer turn and dart back into the trees. That was when the rage really began. The flip was switched, and the ever-more fragile trigger was pulled. The real Wallace came to light. The monster behind the mask. It was the Wallace the kids knew, the one they lived with, and the one they feared.

Matt knew something was coming. He could sense it the way an animal can sense a thunderstorm. His natural urge was to run, to find shelter from said storm. He let go of the gun and jumped to his feet. He turned and made a run for it, but Wallace was already holding onto the back of his shirt.

"You let him get away. All you had to do was pull the god-forsaken trigger and we would be done with all this girly shite. You are a boy, almost a man. By the time I was your age, I was hunting with my dad, not under his watch." Wallace's face had turned a thunderous shade of purple and his temper exploded, boiling over. It was driven by a sense of failure. His son had failed him, and he too had failed. Wallace had failed himself, and he could not hold his disappointment in anymore. He tightened his grip on Matt's arm and began to shake him back and forth. He would not stop, and as Matt's cries rang out, doubtlessly drawing the attention of every hunter, hiker, and trail blazer in the vicinity, it was Levi who came to his brother's aid.

"Dad, that's enough. Dad!" He took hold of his father's arms and disengaged him from his brother. "He's sorry. Besides, don't you think it was a big target for his first kill?" Levi talked to his father, calming him down. "Let's head back to camp. We have more than enough to take home and keep the fridge full all winter. Matt will do better next time, won't you, Matt?" Levi spoke to his brother, but did not move from his position, square on against his father.

"I will. I promise I will." Matt was quick to agree, even if his tears had not yet stopped. He took quick ragged gulps of air as he tried to calm himself.

"Whatever. I'm done with him. I won't bring him next year. It's just you and me, Levi, the men of the family," Wallace scoffed, shaking himself free from his eldest son's grasp. He turned and walked away, knowing his children would fall in line behind him.

"Are you okay?" Levi asked, once his father was out of earshot. Even as the favourite son, he was fearful of his father's temper, and far from immune to his wrath.

"I'm fine," Matt sniveled, walking after his father.

They walked back to camp in silence. Their father's rage still fouled the air. The trail was thick with it, like the air after a jet plane had flown over head.

Neither boy truly believed that it would be their final camping trip together. As it would happen, it turned out to be their final month together.

Once they got back home, with Matt having been ignored for the remainder of the trip, their mother immediately noticed the tension between them. The relationship between father and youngest son had never been the strongest, and the years were peppered with disagreements, but there was something different this time. A sense of finality that everybody recognized and had seen coming, but all refused to acknowledge, at least before it was too late.

The bruises on Matt's arms had been at the height of their thunderous colouration when their mother Elaine had seen them.

Matt didn't need to say anything for her to piece together what had happened. The ensuing fight between her and her drunken husband had ended badly. He had pulled his service revolver, and unloaded as it was, it was the final straw in a relationship that had been flooded with physical and mental abusive for several decades.

Elaine had moved out that night, while her husband nursed the black eye she gave him for pulling the gun. She had taken Matt with her, and within two weeks divorce papers had been served. Levi had already moved out of the family home and was living in a flat with a couple of other rookie officers from the academy. Far from ignorant to his father's problems, Levi remained close with both parents, but never saw them in the same room again. At least not for over two decades.

***

APPLETON, WISCONSIN,
JUNE, 2015

Matt Carmichael pulled his car into the lot and shut off the engine. The summer weather soon made the small vehicle oppressively hot. Sweat glistened on his brow, yet Matthew, for that was the name he went by now, just couldn't seem to get warm. He cupped his hands and blew into them. It had been seven years since he had seen the rest of his family. He didn't want to admit it, as it made the circumstances of his return all the more painful.

Getting out of the car, he took a deep breath and walked up to the building. There was a scattering of cars in the lot, but not enough.In his mind it should have been full; people parking on the streets in order to get one final chance of saying goodbye. Still, he could not control the actions of others. People had become desensitized by death.

A doorman greeted him. He was dressed in a black suit, white shirt and black tie. He held a hat in his hands, which when he was not opening and closing the door for the mourners, was held low, crossed before his body.

"Thank you," Matt spoke softly.

"My condolences for your loss," the man answered. It was a rehearsed line, one used daily. Nothing more than a button on repeat, really, but Matt found a comfort in it that he could never repay.

Walking inside, the heat of the day was lost. The cool air-conditioning made the temperature drop. It did little to take the chill from Matt's body, but it didn't matter. A blazing inferno would not have been enough to warm him, for he knew what lay beyond the doors, and it terrified him.

The room was quiet, laid out in a neat and functional style. The atmosphere was sombre, as to be expected at a funeral.

Elaine lay in the small room to the side of the main chapel. A handful of people were milling about, hovering in the doorway, not willing to cross the threshold and enter the room where death sat stroking the hair of its latest acquisition.

A few people turned his way as Matt moved through them, gliding easily between them all so as to offer no disturbance. Friend, relative, or mere acquaintance, they all had the right to attend, and to mourn as they saw fit.

The room was small, and even cooler than the rest of the building. There were no windows, and only a dull lighting around the edges of the room, save for the lights that hung above the coffin. *All eyes needed to be on the star of the show*. Matt didn't know where the thought came from, or the dark, dry wit it was laced with, but he didn't like it.

His mother lay on the silk-lined padding, her blonde hair a wig, but a near impeccable capture of the way she wore it before cancer stripped her down to flesh upon bone. Her face was smaller than Matt remembered; her whole body seemed to have shrunk. Yet he felt no fear, and even his sorrow ebbed away some when he saw the look of utter peace on her face. She was sleeping, free of the pain that had dominated the final three years of her life. Matt had been there every step of the way, taking her to her doctor's appointments, and making sure that she got the best care he could provide.

In the end, however, Elaine had been determined to die in the place she lived all of her life. A hospice nearby the area she lived as a child had been able to accommodate her, and for the last four months of her life, Elaine had suffered there. The staff had been wonderful, giving Matt daily updates on her condition. The fact that Matt was a doctor no doubt helped, for he insisted they did not sugarcoat the news for him.

Elaine had been a fighter her whole life, from an abusive childhood, to a marriage that she would later admit had been dominated by rage from the moment they met, to the way she fought the aches and pains of aging, and finally the disease that claimed her life.

"It's all over now, Mom," Matt whispered as he leaned over to plant a final kiss on her forehead. Her skin was cool to his lips, while his tears were scalding to his cheeks.

Matt sat with his mother for a time. People left him in peace, and he found comfort in it. It was not this moment that terrified him, nor the inevitable finality of her coffin being lowered into the ground. It was the odds of seeing his brother, Levi, that terrified him. He had not spoken with his brother for several years, their relationship strained by Levi's attachment to his father. Matt could never understand how Levi could love the man that abused them all. It had led to a fight, which had in turn led to a silence that tore what fragile bonds remained in their family apart.

Matt rose and left the room, wiping away his tears. He didn't look at his mother as he walked away, because he knew that one last look, one last moment of comfort sought, would never be enough.

Levi was standing with the minister that was going to conduct the service. They were locked in a deep conversation. Matt thought it would make a great moment to slide into his seat and blend into the crowd. However, the moment he made a move towards the rows of seats, Levi turned around. Their eyes met, and for a moment Matt's heart stopped. His brother looked just like their father. The same facial features and stern expression. The same body language and rapidly receding hairline.

Neither of them moved, and then before they knew it, they were embracing.

"I'm so sorry, brother. I know you were with her through it all," Levi began, and suddenly this embrace felt like a stranglehold, a restraint.

Matt stiffened, prepared to lecture his brother again, to blame him, but as he broke their embrace and saw the pain and sorrow in Levi's eyes, Matt knew that his brother was speaking the truth.

Tears streaked Levi's face and his stern features had melted into those of a lost and scared child.

"I'm sorry for everything, Matt. I've missed you every day." Levi crumbled and fell back into his brother's open arms.

"I know, man. I know." Matt felt his own tears boiling behind his eyes, his head hurt from the pressure of keeping them inside; a promise he had made to himself, but he couldn't fight it any longer. The tears came, and the brothers were reunited.

The service went without a hitch. Matt and Levi talked and reminisced on the good times, the times spent with their mother after the divorce. Neither mentioned their father, not that final hunting trip, yet it was a special time for them, because in spite of what happened, as they walked back, following Wallace's shadow, the two boys had never been closer, and from that day on, all they did was drift slowly further apart.

"Do you fancy grabbing a drink?" Levi asked. He and Matt had walked around after the service, revisiting the places they had spent so many years.

"I don't drink," Matt answered.

"Ok, then I'll buy you a coke, little brother." Levi smiled and put Matt completely at ease.

"Sure thing, detective," Matt joked. "I still can't believe you are a detective," he added only half-heartedly humorous.

The bar *The Jolly Bastard* was quiet, in spite of the external claims for a true Irish experience.

Matt had a bad feeling about the way the afternoon was unfolding, but followed his brother, happy to have somebody by his side.

"Hello, Matt," a voice spoke from behind him. It was a cigarette-cracked voice, deep and gravelled. It was a long way from the voice he remembered, yet Matt knew who it was before he even began to turn around.

"How could you?" Matt looked accusingly at his brother. "This whole thing was a setup." Anger boiled beneath his skin; it consumed him in a flash of blinding white rage. He felt betrayed.

"Matt, he has changed. He wanted to come, to see you, and to say goodbye to Mom." Levi tried to explain but Matt was shaking his head long before his brother finished speaking.

"Son ..." their father began, but Matt refused to turn around and face him.

They stood at the bar, their meeting so awkward that even the barman did not come to interrupt. He stood at the end of the bar by the only other man there, and there would be no serving him either, for his drunken snores were evidence that he had already seen his limit receding in the rear-view mirror.

"You shouldn't have brought him, Levi. Not today, of all days," Matt continued, addressing only his brother, as if it were just the two of them.

"Your mother was the love of my life. Please, Matt, I know I did you wrong. I did you all wrong, but you are my boy. Losing your mother back then didn't wake me up, but losing her now, and knowing how close I could be too, that pains me greatly." There was a hint of honest emotion in his father voice, and for a moment Matt felt his resolve slipping. Then the image of the deer, and the rage at his refusal to kill. He heard his mother's screams as he beat her, while the boys were tucked up in bed at night, supposedly asleep, and suddenly his resolve strengthened again.

"No," Matt spoke and was surprised to find himself weeping.

"Matt, give him a chance. That's all he wants. Please, for me?" Levi asked, his face wrought with emotion. Slowly, Matt turned around and came face to face with the man he had not seen for close to two thirds of his life.

His father had changed a great deal. The broad and powerful man had been replaced by an old one. His body still large and strong, but clearly wracked by the ravages of aging, compounded by a choice of lifestyle that was equally damaging. He stood with a stoop and had a constant wince on his face. Matt knew the look well, and the cause. A slipped disc, maybe two; the lean was prominent enough. His face had sunken, wrinkles destroyed his once strong features. His nose seemed swollen, while both it and his cheeks had a strange purple tint to them, snaked with a road map of red capillaries, pulled to the surface through prolonged alcohol abuse.

A mess of greying beard hung around his mouth and his breathing was slightly laboured, bordering on a wheeze. Yet two things had not changed, or suffered through the years. The stern look in his eyes, and the general aura of anger and hate that he seemed to exude like body odour.

"What do you want?" Matt asked, happy to find his voice so firm.

"I don't want to be your best friend, and I know you don't want me to be your father," he began.

"You got that right," Matt interrupted him.

"Then maybe I could at least be an acquaintance. Maybe get a visit or a call at Christmas. Please, Matt. I've missed you for so much of your life, don't make me miss you for what is left of mine." There was again air of genuine emotion behind the words, but Matt felt on edge by it all.

"Why should I?" Matt found bite in his words, and a strange deep-seated glimmer of joy sparked inside him when he saw the wince his father made at the blatant rejection.

"I can't make you. I really can't, but I am sick, Matt. I've lived a hard life and I ruined yours. Your brother stayed with me, which is more than I deserve. The two of you needed a better father than me, a better role model. I am here to make it up to you. I want to take you on a trip." His father began to cough, lowering his head to his chest as his lungs rattled. Matt thought he saw blood staining his father's fist, but he hid the hand too quick for any certainty.

Matt laughed, and it echoed around the small bar. "I need a drink." He turned around and looked at the barman who came their way with a look of consternation on his face. He would not be hanging around looking for conversation, that much was obvious.

"Can I have a beer?" Matt asked.

"I thought you didn't drink?" Levi jumped in.

"There are always extenuating circumstances, you must understand that, Detective." The humour was gone from his use of the word, but the snide nature of his enunciation made it hurt.

"I'll take one too," Levi offered, smiling at his brother, ignoring the barbed comment. He understood what he was going through.

"I'll go for the same, and this one is on me," Wallace spoke up. Matt didn't offer anything else. He knew it made him a hypocrite, but he didn't care.

The barman delivered their drinks, took their money and promptly left them to their own devices once more.

"Why do you think I would go on a trip with you?" Matt asked, picking up their conversation without missing a beat. There were a few more people in the bar now, the lunch traffic had started to arrive, but they all gave the three men a wide berth.

"I don't expect anything, but well, I remember you were always such a softie. You loved the outdoors and animals. I wanted to try and make it up to you by taking the two of you away, on a sort of safari," Wallace spoke, his breathing growing more laboured.

"You just don't give up, do you?" Matt snapped, slamming his beer down on the bar top. "What's it been, twenty-three years, something like that, and the first thing you ask me, the first goddamned thing, is if I want to go hunting with you?" Matt felt the blood rushing to his face. His vision darkened and spittle flew from his lips.

"Who said anything about hunting? I mean a real safari, in Africa. Your mother dying made me realize things, and well … I want to make it up to you." Wallace looked close to dropping to his knees and pleading. His beer was still untouched. Matt could not recall having ever seen him look so vulnerable.

"What makes you think I would even consider it?" Matt asked. Truth be told, a safari was his dream holiday, and one he had been planning for in his mind for many years. Only, he was finally approaching the end of his medical residency and had neither the time nor the money to take such a trip.

"I don't expect you would." Wallace sounded defeated. "However, if you choose to join us, the ticket is right here." He reached into his pocket and pulled out an envelope. He placed it on the bar and slid it towards Matt. Wallace said nothing else, but picked up his beer, drained the glass in one attempt, and then left.

The bar was busier now, and the moment Wallace left, it was as if the sound returned to the world. The clatter of glasses and the hushed chatter of multiple conversations mingling into one constant stream of words that nobody could make sense of.

Matt and Levi stood in silence for a moment, allowing the growing atmosphere of the bar to wash over them.

"Is he serious?" Matt looked at his brother, his eyes searching for an answer.

"About the holiday, yes. He gave me my ticket last week. The safari part was new to me." Levi smiled as he took a drink of his beer.

"Not just about that. I meant is he serious about being different?" Matt noticed how Levi took a slow intake of breath before answering.

"He isn't the same as he was back then," Levi answered.

Matt didn't believe him.

CHAPTER 3

SOMEWHERE, AFRICA
MAY 2015

As was becoming customary in the underground laboratory, the scream rang out and fell suddenly silent. There was a wet crunch followed by a juicy bursting sound.

In the six months that had passed since their original Spider breakthrough, Julian and Tracy had become somewhat numb to the occurrences. The screams blended into the sounds of the world they had helped invade. It helped that they were worlds apart, separated by a barrier that they controlled and could close at any minute.

While the screams could be forced into the background, what neither of them could ignore was the fact that the number of bodies brought back came nowhere near to the total number of men lost. In the six months that had passed since Albert Wilhelm III wheeled himself into their lives, more than fifty others had lost theirs.

Julian and Tracy were happy that their duties had been limited to monitoring and maintaining the Spider. They had learned early on to ignore the equipment and boxes that were passed through on a daily basis. They knew what was beyond the Spider's core, they would never forget what they saw that first day, but they knew nothing about the true horrors of the world, and had no intention of finding out.

The same could not be said for Luc. Since Albert's arrival, they had hardly seen their friend. He had been whisked away to a different lab, a separate section of the same underground complex. When they did see him, Luc was quiet and sullen. He withdrew from them, eating at a different table, and for a while even at different times. He had grown a dark beard which covered the lower half of his face, and looked for all intents and purposes like a man with the weight of the world on his shoulders.

It had only been in recent weeks that he had re-joined them. He was often quiet and sullen, but they did, not push him. The underground facility felt oddly crowded with the construction crew moved in. Private conversations were easily overheard, but after a while nobody cared. People were too wrapped up in their own pain to worry about that of another. It came as a complete surprise therefore, when Luc turned to them one day and passed a note across the table top. He looked at both Julian and Tracy in turn, words not needed to voice his instructions. He rose from the table and left before they reached for the note.

It was a scrap of graphical paper, and all that it contained was a time, 21:45, written in black marker.

Julian pocketed the note and left with Tracy on his heels. None of them trusted Albert, and knew without need for explanation that his two bodyguards were bad news. They looked as if they would happily kill the trio with or without Albert's consent. Their fear turned to mistrust when attention was directed to the other members of staff; the construction crew were all ex-marines, several of them eyed Luc with a certain degree of fear and hatred; recognition based on past deeds. They could not be trusted, and so any conversations that broached the subject of Albert's true intentions needed to be strategically timed.

Julian, Tracy, and Luc knew every inch of the facility, including the corridors that had not been marked on the map given to them upon their arrival. It was easy for them to understand the note Luc had passed them. He had something they needed to hear, but something he clearly did not want to risk having overheard by ears that may not be fully impartial.

The small empty room was located along the east side rear corridor. It was a service route that had long since been closed off. However, inquisitive minds left to their own devices can easily overcome the issue of a simple lock, and so the trio had learned every inch of the maintenance passageways that ringed the entire complex. There were many places they could meet, but the room in question was easily accessible to them all from either their quarters, the dining area, or the main lab.

Luc was already waiting for them when they got to the room. He was pacing around nervously. They had never seen him nervous before.

"Luc, what is it?" Tracy asked once they had the door closed and were certain that they were alone.

"This place. We need to find a way to stop it." Luc stopped pacing. He had a look in his eyes; the glare of a condemned man. A man who was backed into a corner and had no way of fighting back out.

"What is it?" Julian asked, stepping forward, subconsciously moving between his oldest friend and the woman he loved.

"Julian, I've done a lot of things in my time. Things I would rather never speak of again and have no intention of doing. I've worked for some very bad men, but none have scared me as much as this Wilhelm guy." The fear in Luc's words was genuine.

"Why, what's he doing with the Spider, do you know?" Tracy stepped forward. She knew who Luc was, but was not afraid of him.

"I can't say. If you knew, they would know it. It's not safe here. There are people on his crew that recognize me. They will kill me the first chance they get." Luc paused, searching for the right words.

"Nobody would do that in here. There is no way. We are all on top of each other, practically under watch twenty-four seven," Tracy offered, hoping to cheer Luc up, but his face didn't change.

"He's not talking about in here," Julian interrupted. "You mean out there, don't you?" Julian looked at Luc, reading him as best he could. "They are sending you through the Spider."

"No, they can't. Why? What is this all about?" The questions that they had all been asking themselves repeatedly over the last six months, came in a tirade.

"Wilhelm is a powerful man. He has more money than there is a number to define. He heard of the Spider programme, and bought it. He didn't just sponsor it, he fucking bought it. That machine out there, the work you are doing, have done. He owns it." Luc didn't rush his story even though he knew they were pushed for time. He needed them to understand what was happening.

"He can't. That's not possible," Julian stammered.

"It's true." Luc stared at his friend. "He owns everything, us included. He needs me to go through because I know too much, and he needs to have me taken care of."

The finality of the words echoed around the empty room. A standard acoustic effect, but one they had not noticed until that moment.

"Then why go?" Tracy asked, refusing to see the futility in at least proposing the idea of a counter argument.

"I don't have a choice, but don't worry, Tracy, I won't go down without a fight." Luc tried a smile, but managed nothing more than a twitch on the left side of his mouth.

"What is he up to? Tell us, maybe we can help," Julian asked. He would not let his friend walk to his death.

"I can't tell you. If I did, then he would know and kill you too. Everybody who knows about this place will be killed. There can be no survivors outside his own group. He has too much at stake to risk the truth getting out."

"Listen, we all know what is through there. We saw it." Julian began to mount his counteroffensive conversation trajectory, but Luc stopped him immediately.

"You have no idea. He's had me working on things in the other lab. Weapons and the like. You could not even fathom the world that lies beyond. He isn't using the Spider for science, and he is not using it for war. He is far more dangerous than that," Luc said.

"Then what?" Tracy asked, rapt in the conversation like a kid listening to stories of years gone by.

"Greed, pure and simple greed. He is a rich man who has found a way to make even more money. Of all the people I have known, and had the displeasure of working for, or against, the ones driven by financial gain that are the coldest, and most evil of them all." Luc looked around nervously, suddenly fearful that their location was not as secure as they had allowed themselves to believe. "We can't stay here any longer. They know every inch of this place." Luc paused. "I love you guys." He sniffed and left the room before either of them could begin any protracted and emotional goodbyes.

Julian and Tracy stood in silence, listening to Luc's footsteps fade away, and then suddenly fall silent as the door to the room closed, sealing them inside.

Tracy began to sob.

The next morning was uneventful. The first shift went through the Spider, and as was customary, the first ten seconds were greeted with a frozen silence in the lab. They had learned fast that the first ten seconds often laid the foundation or a good or a bad day.

No screams came, and so slowly, everybody got back to work.

"Prepare the Spider for transport," the weaselly voice of Albert Wilhelm III echoed across the silent lab. As always, he seemed to emerge from the shadows, only after his audience had reacted.

"You want us to bring them back already?" Julian asked, feigning surprise. The truth was, he had been expecting the request, going about his task waiting for the order to come.

"No, Dr. Grau, we have another load to send through," Albert answered a little too quickly. "I want to prepare you both, for your friend Luc will be making the trip. His skills are required on the other side. We have entered the final phase now. In another week or two, we will be open for business." Albert smiled. On many people, a smile changed their face for the better, their eyes glistened with the happiness their mouth conveyed. Not Albert. His smile was cold and snake-like. His eyes did not glisten as much as reflect the light of the room, as if they were mirrors rather than windows.

Beside him, Julian felt Tracy stiffen. He reached out and touched her leg, a small subtle gesture but it was enough to convey his message. She relaxed, and Julian heard her shuddered breaths as she tried to control herself.

"Very well. Luc is a good man, he will be fine out there," Julian answered, hoping he had not given too much away.

"Yes, we will see. It is a dangerous world out there." Albert stretched his snake-like smile across his features once more and then left. He was never one to hang around, and could never be seen or sought at any point in time. His appearances and involvement was fully at his own discretion.

A few minutes later, the second load of the day arrived. Three military men armed with AK-47s along with holstered pistols, and hunting knives strapped to their lower legs, were well prepared. Luc was unarmed, or so it appeared. He was pushing a trolley laden with four large boxes. He looked at Julian and Tracy as he walked, doing so with his eyes only, for moving his head and making a visible gesture was too dangerous.

Julian heard Tracy's stifled sobs. Julian nodded to his friend, and the same gesture was returned. As Luc stepped through the Spider's red energy core, Julian felt his own eyes mist. Luc was gone without so much as a final goodbye or a wave. The three military men followed him, and in the lab, the wait began.

One …

Two …

Three …

Four …

Five … Julian counted, unaware that he was doing so aloud. Then it came. The single gunshot that they had been waiting for. It seemed to echo around the room, booming the announcement that the job was done. A puff of blue steel smoke wafted through the Spider, bringing with it the acrid aroma of a gun's discharge.

Tracy fell into the chair, her sobs hidden, wept into the crook of her elbow, but inconsolable nonetheless. Julian felt numb. His mind raced, filled with unanswered questions. Questions he knew he could never ask, questions he feared he already knew some of the answers to. Julian knew he could weep, openly mourn his friend, but instead he re-grouped, promising himself the freedom to grieve once he was back in his room.

Turning back to the console, he checked the dials and made a fresh note in the logs. The Spider was holding steady.

CHAPTER 4

BLOEMFONTEIN, SOUTH AFRICA
JULY 2015

The three men stood at the baggage carousel waiting for their bags to arrive. To anybody else waiting, they would have looked like three strangers waiting for their bags, standing side by side through coincidence. Only the facial similarities between Wallace and Levi could have made them consider the two were connected through more than their choice of travel company and destination.

For a long time, it looked as though Matt would not turn up. He had not spoken to his father or brother since the funeral, and while the pair waited at the gate for the first of three flights to their final destination, there was neither hide nor hair of Matt.

He had arrived, later than them but in plenty of time for the flight, but he chose to sit and wait out of sight, moving at the last possible moment to head to his seat. The three men were seated side by side, separated by an aisle.

Matt quickly claimed the solo seat, planted the headphones over his ears and picked up a book. It was a medical text and more than enough to get him through the flight without having to converse with anybody.

With their bags collected, it was onwards towards the exit. Moving through the ever-watchful eyes of customs, the three men continued to move in silence. They seemed to be the first people to leave the baggage hall, at least the only ones to do so via the left-hand exit. The electronic doors opened and the silence of the hall, with its jetlagged passengers and sombre airport staff, was replaced by the hustle and bustle of an active airport. The wall of noise hit them harder than it should have. The wail of infants, their patience finally worn thin, either from having just gotten off the plane or through waiting to collect someone else. The tears of joy after being reunited with loved ones and the general squeals of happiness.

"Where are the taxis?" Levi asked as they stood on the other side. They had officially arrived. Their holiday could begin.

"I don't think we need to worry about that," Matt offered, pointing forward to where the short, smartly dressed chauffeur stood holding a sign that read their names.

"Would you look at that?" Wallace whistled as they walked up to the man. Wallace was the freshest out of all of them. Having spent the first half of the flight drinking somewhat heavily, he had then fallen into a deep sleep, his snores overpowering even the whine of the engines on the small jet that had taken them on the final leg of their journey.

"Good afternoon, gentlemen. If you would follow me, there is a car waiting for you," the young man spoke with a heavy accent, but at the same time was easy to understand. He turned with a soldier's precision and marched away, leading the Carmichael family to the waiting limousine.

"Is this your first time visiting?" he asked as he instructed the airport porter to load their bags into the car. The man, whose skin was as dark as fresh pitch loaded the car with a smile and walked away without so much as asking for a tip.

"Yes, it is our first time outside of the US," Wallace answered.

"Yours maybe." Matt couldn't help but offer the sharp reply.

The limousine was enormous, and could have held another six or seven fully grown men before space even began to be a problem. Yet, the three men sat together, Wallace already exploring the bar, pulling out the drinks he wanted, and opening them all one after another.

"You gentlemen are in for quite the treat." The voice of their driver floated from the speakers that were embedded around the ceiling of the vehicle. "You are the very first guests to be accepted to the Wilhelm Big Game Safari. Your names will be written into the history books," the driver continued. "The journey will take us about two hours, so sit back and enjoy the food and drink. If I can be of any service, just push the green button located in the door panel."

The voice faded and the sounds of the MP3 selection Matt had chosen as soon as he got into the elongated car began again.

"Big Game, huh," Matt spoke, eyeing his father, sizing him up the way a boxer studied his opponent before a fight. The distrust must have been clear on his face, because his father knew exactly what he was trying to say.

"Now, Matt. I told you we were going on safari, and that is exactly what we are going to do." Wallace smiled at his son, which only served to add to the tension that had filled the back of the car.

The two-hour trip passed at a snail's pace, with conversation kept to a minimum. Matt read his texts, and Wallace drank. When any form of communication was needed between any of the parties, it was done so through Levi, who was already growing tired of both his father and his brother.

"Oh for Pete's sake. Will you two stop acting like babies? Matt, if you were just going to cause trouble, why the heck did you get on that damned plane." Levi's voice was raised, but he did a good job of keeping his anger down. It was the voice of a cop, there could be no doubt about that. "And Dad, why don't you just tell Matt …" Levi stopped when the limousine pulled to a stop.

They heard the driver close his door and ten seconds later their door was opened. Heat streamed into the car. Getting out felt the same way it did getting into a car in the middle of summer. It was not a horrid feeling, but it would take some getting used to.

"What were you about to say, Levi?" Matt looked at his brother, his rage still boiling. "He should man up and tell me …"Matt pushed to hear his father admit what he already suspected to be the case, but for the second time in a few minutes they were interrupted.

"Welcome, gentlemen. It is an honour to have you here as the first ever guests at the Wilhelm Big Game reserve." The voice carried across the parking lot they had stopped in. It took a few moments before any of them saw the man in the wheelchair slowly making his way towards them. He was a small man, his skin a shade of pasty that bordered on translucent. A sickly sweat seemed to cover his body, plastering his hair to his head.

"It's a pleasure to be here." Levi stepped forward to take control of the conversation. His father was in no condition, and his brother was not thinking clearly. "It's been a long trip, could we maybe freshen up at the hotel before we have orientation or whatever?" Levi asked, studying the man. The man put Levi on edge. There was something about him, the dark, cold eyes and the near sinister expression his face wore when he smiled.

"Of course, my apologies. It has been a long flight for you all," the man began, reversing his wheelchair as he prepared to turn. "Allow me to introduce myself and explain the rules very briefly. My name is Albert Wilhelm III, and this is my safari. Please, refrain judgement until you have seen the wildlife side of the center. This building is a scientific research laboratory, and should you so wish, I could arrange a tour for you. It really is quite impressive. Your quarters are located below ground, on this site."

"You mean there's no hotel?" Wallace growled from behind Levi.

"No, there is no hotel. But we do have room and board, three meals a day, and the lower floors have been remodelled to give guests that same hotel feeling. All we ask is that you stay on your allocated floor. The research staff here work around the clock, and to disturb them would not be recommended. It is only for one night, for after that you shall head out into the wild." The man turned his chair, but was not finished just yet. "One more thing, gentlemen, no alcohol will be allowed on the premises. I hope you understand."

"Yes, sir, we do," Matt was quick to reply, throwing a quick glance towards his father.

"Very well, those are the rules. Follow me, and I will take you to your quarters."

They walked after the man in the wheelchair. They crossed the parking lot and headed towards a large building that had more window than brickwork, at least on the wall facing them. The rays of the sun glistened on their surface. Matt wondered how hot it must get for those sitting behind them. As they drew closer, he saw they were not windows, but solar panels.

The entrance to the building was a plain set of double doors. They were met by a security guard who wrote them into the books and provided them the passes they would need to move around. Albert was joined by two large men in suits. They said nothing but walked behind his chair. Matt could see the weapons they had hidden in the waistband of their trousers. A sense of apprehension was growing inside him, and it was becoming more of a concern than his father's anticipated lies.

"Gentlemen, unfortunately my presence is required in one of our laboratories. My associates here will see you to your rooms. Get some rest, freshen up, and I will have you notified when the evening meal is ready. I assure you of both my presence and undivided attention. We have much to discuss. This is going to be very exciting indeed. You men are about to become part of history." There was a genuine delight to Albert's voice, a keenness, yet Matt could not shake the seedy echo the words seemed to leave behind.

The lift took them down an unknown number of floors. The button was not labelled. There was only one, so the need for such identification was moot.

Matt felt his ears pop as they descended. He could smell the alcoholic stench of his father standing beside him. He wanted to move, the lift was more than spacious enough, but the presence of the armed guards held him still.

The feeling of unease grew in Matt's belly the deeper they sank. When the doors finally opened, the cool, air-conditioned atmosphere that hit them was a stark contrast to what they had felt above ground.

The guards said nothing as they led them down the corridor. Doors lined either side, and with the white-tiled walls and the dark-coloured floor, coupled with the exposed lighting and lack of any real decorating skill beyond the functional, there was little to make them feel as if they were being led to their accommodation. They could just as easily be being led to room 101, where their greatest fears came to life.

"This is yours." The guard's voice was gruff and he spoke so suddenly that the accent on his words was lost to Matt.

"Thank you," Matt answered, his response sounding close to a question.

The guard said nothing as he unlocked the door, and handed Matt a key card. "This will get you access to the areas you need. Meals are served three times a day, and we will collect you when it is time; however, you are free to use the secondary canteen one floor down whenever you would like. Take the stairs." The voice alternated from sounding like the perfect hospitality clerk to that of an angry old man growling at kids who keep stepping on his lawn.

The room was large and airy, and clearly not historically a location used for sleeping. There was a large double bed, and a giant flat screen television on the wall opposite hanging above a long desk. There was a table and two chairs, and a rug on the floor. The furnishings were nice, and looked to be of a high quality, but nothing belonged together. The wood of the bed, table, and TV unit did not match in shade or tree. The rug had been laid down to distract from the cold, tiled floor. There was no central bathroom, but as Matt looked around he found the plan of the guest lodgings and saw three bathrooms were located on each of the two floors.

Sitting on the bed, he found it surprisingly firm. Laying back he let out a sigh and instantly felt sleep coming for him. Not bothering to undress, Matt hauled himself further onto the bed and slipped into a deep slumber.

He woke a time later. How much later he did not know, because there was no clock in the room. Sitting up, refreshed from his nap but still not fully awake, Matt fumbled with the remote and eventually got the TV working. The picture was bright and the volume boomed. Turning it down, he tried to find the guide. Only, it was not the sort of TV that offered entertainment. It was an introduction video and a guide.

The image of Albert Wilhelm III came into view. He was sitting in the jungle, or so it looked. Matt took one look and knew that it was nothing but trickery. The colours were too vivid, and the density of the foliage suggested a depth that would have been impassable for a wheelchair.

"Hello, welcome to the Wilhelm Big Game Reserve. In this interactive guide, you will learn more about the work we are doing here, the scientific research and the various projects we are working on with regards re-habitation and breeding of some of the most majestic big game creatures the world has ever seen." Albert's image faded out of view and it was replaced with a cinematic reel of science labs and fertility labs. A strange music played in the background.

Albert reappeared. "In the coming screens, you can learn more about the reserve, and with the special menu at the end of this presentation, you will be given the ability to choose which of our big game creatures you are most interested in hunting." The word made Matt's blood freeze in his veins.

Rage boiled up inside him, as he recalled his father's repeated lies. He zoned out from the voice on the television that was talking about weapons. The guns didn't look like anything Matt had ever seen before, but he was too irate to worry about the guns he would not be firing.

Rage consumed him. Matt turned the TV off, grabbed the clean shirt he had been in the process of donning when Albert's video had distracted him, and stormed towards the door. Wrenching it open, he had every intention of finding his father and doing something unimaginable. He was not expecting to find a large, armed guard standing with his fist raised.

The fist was in preparation for the knock on the door that would have preceded the call to dinner, but to Matt it looked like the man was moving to hit him. He jumped backwards with a cry. He stared at the man who, although he hid it well, looked just as shocked.

"I've been sent to bring you to dinner. We will eat on the fourteenth floor. It is a restricted area, so please remain by my side at all times." The man spoke without making any true eye contact with Matt. It was a trait that Matt found unnerving.

It was evident that verbal communication was not required, and that suited Matt fine. He followed the man, silently stewing in his own rage.

The lift stopped and Matt was as good as shoved out through the doors before they had finished opening. The set-up of the room made Matt think of a school canteen, plastic tables and chairs clustered in groups, a scuffed linoleum floor. Matt looked around. He was the first to arrive. He could see that there was an alcove to the left where under any other circumstances than this, food would be served in the typical school dinner style. He could almost smell the bulk-cooked meals. He could hear the wet slop they made as portions were spooned onto plates.

In the center of the canteen, a table had already been made up. Matt took his seat, picking the spot that gave him a good view of the lifts. It didn't take long before the doors issued a shrill ping and pulled back, revealing the two other members of his party.

Wallace and Levi appeared in deep conversation. They had both showered and changed; Wallace even looked sober. Both men laughed together and neither looked at Matt.

If they had, they would have telegraphed what was coming. Matt was not a violent man, and so his punch was obvious; his fist was cocked before he had taken his first step. Nonetheless, it was thrown with force, catching Wallace as he raised his head. The fist drove into his face, and Matt felt the cartilage of his father's nose crunch beneath his blow. Blood flowed from the injured, if not broken, body part. Matt felt a surge of relief rush through him. He screamed in rage as he felt the cathartic benefit of the altercation, and imagined that was how a junkie must have felt taking a hit. A sudden, all-encompassing feeling of peace swept through his body. It was followed up by a second wave as he saw his father stumble backwards, tripping over his own feet as he moved. Wallace crashed into the table behind him and as a result fell onto his ass, sending the table scooting across the floor and the chairs flying in all directions.

He stared up at his son, rage in his eyes, but Levi was quicker than his father and moved between the two. "I take it you watched the intro screen, little brother." He too spoke with a sneer.

"You knew all along, didn't you?" His rage now directed towards his brother.

"Yes, but it's …" Levi began and Matt moved in to strike him also.

"Gentlemen, I hope everything is to your liking," their host's voice called out, rising above their own argument.

It was a voice that stopped them in their tracks. They looked around, and at first they could not see their host. He appeared the second time their eyes scanned the room, his chair working its way through the tables and chairs.

"I do trust that this familial quarrel will not change anything regarding this trip. All of the arrangements have been made. It would be a shame, not to mention a waste of your money, to have one of your party leave." Albert smiled at them, that same reptilian smile that kept Julian and Tracy so on edge.

"No, no it's nothing. Is it, Matt?" Levi spoke, facing his brother, his expression stern.

Matt paused. He didn't know what to say. He kept his eyes locked on Wallace. He no longer saw the man as his father, or even somebody worthy of the moniker. He saw him for the lying, abusive drunk he always was. "No, no problem here," Matt answered and he meant it. It surprised him at first, and it was only after he was sitting at the table that he realized why. His subconscious had known the answer before his conscious brain did, but that didn't matter. The wheels had been set in motion.

The meal was a good hearty one, the food not stunning but wholesome and tasty. Wallace was disappointed that there was not even wine with the meal, but a kick from Levi was enough to bring the older man back under control.

"What time do we leave tomorrow?" Levi asked, as he mopped the gravy from his plate with a piece of fresh white bread.

Albert looked at the men around the table. His eyes lingering on each one in turn. "The transport is a simple matter. I think an early start would be the best, give you the most time on the first day. You will need to set up camp and find your bearings, of course. Shall we say a gathering at eight?" He let the offer sit.

"Will we be going in alone?" It was Matt who seemed to be showing the most interest in the conversation.

"No, you will not be going in alone. A team of my associates will accompany you. You will find weapons waiting for you on the other side. Once you have arrived in the reserve, how you go about your hunt is entirely your own prerogative. Whether you stay as a group, or each go your own way, as long as you are together in three days' time. We will not wait for anybody that does not make it to the rendezvous point in time for extraction," Albert instructed.

The table was quiet. Each for different reasons, but quiet all amounted to the same net result. Silence. All that could be heard was the occasional creak from the wheelchair.

"It was an enjoyable meal, gentlemen, and a pleasure spending time with you. I must now get back to the labs; there is always much work to be done here, as I am sure you can understand. I would strongly suggest that you get some rest also. Tomorrow we make history." With nothing more to be said, Albert turned his wheelchair and left.

The three men were collected, and escorted back to their rooms. Matt couldn't help but feel as if he were being held captive, rather than hosted.

Matt didn't sleep much. The bed was delightful, firm yet comfortable. The blankets were adequate and there was no irritating clack of traffic or a rattling air-conditioning system. Sleep simply eluded him for the most part of the night. He would doze, falling into semi-slumber, but find himself pulled awake again. Not through bad dreams, but a mixture of memories and a turmoil of emotion regarding every aspect of his life.

It would have been easy for Matt to write off the episode as being a case of nerves before heading out on the safari. The memories of hunting with his father were forever burned into his mind, but it was not the case. Matt had suffered with sleep issues as good as from the day he and his mother left their father and Levi behind. There were good and bad periods, sometimes as much as months between an episode, but they were always there.

The morning broke, and after showering and dressing in the camouflaged clothes that had been provided by the facility, Matt was collected by the same stone-faced guard and escorted to the lift. They stood in silence, his father and brother once again being brought via separate channels. *Maybe they know*, Matt thought, but he quashed it as soon as it flitted through his mind.

The elevator began to move, and to Matt's surprise fell even deeper beneath the surface. The doors opened, and after a short corridor, he was brought into an enormous warehouse area. It made him think of an old school gymnasium, only twice the size and twice as empty. The walls were white, the floor was dark, black or blue, he couldn't be sure, but it was the same colour he had seen everywhere else.

To the right stood an area of computer monitors that lined the walls and multiple terminals stood in grouped clusters. There were two scientists who appeared to be running the whole thing. They moved between the consoles, skirting around each other with a fluidity that showed their connection. They worked in perfect tandem.

To the left stood a group of men, dressed the same as Matt's guard. It took a moment before he realized that he was dressed the same. Although the quality of their military clothing looked far sturdier than his own. Not to mention the thick vests they wore and the automatic rifles they had slung over their shoulders. The soldiers, for that was what they were, laughed and joked. Yet there was a nervous air that hung in the large lab like a cloud of smog over London.

"Wait here," the guard instructed and left Matt standing before the main item in the room: an enormous metallic structure with eight arms that curled upwards towards one another. There was a flight of steps that took them to the base of the platform, but from his position he could see the fittings where the curled arms would normally be held in place. He understood nothing about what he saw, but knew that it was the device that would take them to the safari.

Once Wallace and Levi had joined him, arriving together as they had done with dinner, the soldiers turned their way. It was as if they had only just noticed their presence.

A round of instructions followed, barked like orders by one of the soldiers. "You will keep your weapons on safety the entire time. For your own safety, as well as enjoyment, you will only fire from designated live-fire areas. Do I make myself clear?" He looked at the three men, but posed them no questions. He also did not wait for an answer, their agreement was implied, and would be enforced regardless. The soldier stepped back in line with the others. It was Albert's turn to speak, and he took his time doing so. He positioned his wheelchair and waited, watching the group, allowing the anticipation to build.

"We have two different weapons for you within the reserve, set up at different areas, so while you can take the same weapon with you it is not required. There will be a lot of walking involved, and lugging those weapons along with your own camping gear is just not recommended," Albert spoke.

"What sort of weapons?" Wallace asked, his interest piqued. He had been sober over twelve hours now, and while his drinking was not necessarily serious enough for him to show any physical signs of withdrawal, the mental toll was guaranteed.

"I am glad you asked," Albert spoke again. "We have high-powered large calibre rifles and also a collection of compressed energy rifles. These are unlike anything you will have fired before." The gleam in his eyes was so strong it was startling.

"Alright, now we are talking," Levi said, taking the chance to express his glee.

"Perfect. Well, lastly, let me introduce the team who have made all of this possible. Dr. Grau, Ms. van der Meer, would you come and join us please?" Albert raised his hands in a visual signal of his growing impatience.

The two scientists walked over to the group. They both wore the stereotypical white jackets that helped to define their occupation.

"Gentlemen, meet the minds behind the Spider, the machine you are about to use. Upon your return, if you have and questions that you wish to ask, I will ensure that both of these fine people are free to answer them." Albert clapped his hand, even in the good acoustic atmosphere of the room his impact was weak, but they all knew what it meant.

"Well then, Dr. Grau, if you would be so kind, fire this puppy up and let's get the first ever Wilhelm Safari trip on the road, what do you guys say?"

There were no objections, but now that everything was real, Matt also noticed that there was a clear lack of enthusiasm among the group. In fact, both his father and Levi looked paler than normal.

A few moments later, the Spider came to life. The long, heavy legs rose further upward, until their tips were almost touching.

"I see where they get the name from," Levi joked.

The electricity began to build, blue sparks at first, and then red. The colours mixed until the red grew dominant. The blue faded away, and the central energy core began to build. The three men stood in silence, perplexed by what they were witnessing. Even Wallace could not find the right word to utter in an attempt to ruin the mood.

They were lost to the sight of the red energy core, which had grown to fill the space created by the curled legs of the Spider. The three men were shoved roughly to get them moving.

Their fear was matched by the draw of the core. The energy ball seemed to force everything to gravitate towards it. So much so that none of the men were truly aware that they were passing through the barrier. Not until it was too late.

CHAPTER 5

WILHELM SAFARI RESERVE
LOCATION UNKNOWN

Moving through the energy field was a strange and disorienting experience. A wave of pressure so cold, it felt as if their insides had been frozen. The red energy core became their world, and while it consumed their vision for only a moment, it was enough to leave them blinded by their arrival.

Matt, Levi, and Wallace went first, and were soon joined by the five heavily armed men who would be their guides.

The trained men settled down to business immediately, fanning out in what would have been a circle, had there been a few more people in their group. They all unslung their rifles and stood in a crouch, the butts of their weapons nestled into their shoulders.

For the other three, the experience of a Spider transport was more lasting. Levi crouched down on his haunches, his head in his hands. He retched but managed to restrain from showering the floor with vomit. Wallace was breathing heavily, his face redder than usual, and the purple colouration of his face caused it to glow.

Matt was relatively chipper. His stomach was a little uneasy, and his head spun, but not worse than coming off a carnival ride. Matt's attention was more taken by their surroundings. They were outside, in a world he knew was not their own. The sky above them was a hazy orange. Behind him a mountain rose high into the air. Their arrival had been close to the mountain's base, on a platform that looked equal in construction to the base of the Spider, only minus the arms.

"Where are we?" Matt asked, looking around, trying to fathom how they had created something like this. It was unlike any place he had ever seen, and to have accessed it via a device buried deep below the surface, was almost too much for him to take.

"Welcome to the reserve, boys. Grab your things, we have a good trek to the first point. We're hunting big game now, so get your game faces on, ladies," the guard from the front of the pack called. Having found no immediate threat, they had turned their circle into an arrowhead formation.

Matt stared at the weapons that were sitting in a trunk. It had been locked by a fingerprint scan, opened only by the lead guard. Wallace immediately grabbed the bolt action rifle with what appeared to be a form of night scope attached to it. Levi opted for the Holland and Holland .375 Magnum. It was a brand new weapon, and Levi nodded approvingly as he turned it in his hands. Matt, who had not held a gun since the final hunting trip with his father, looked at the weapons in the box and saw nothing but death on each and every one of them. He could feel the potential for dealing out the end of life and it scared him. It terrified him in a way that it never did when he was a kid. Back then his convictions were strong; he was largely untainted by the world. Now, as an adult, fully used to seeing the barbaric side of man from the inside of a hospital emergency room, he held a new fear, and as much as he refuted it, a fascination for the things. He reached in and pulled out a strange-looking silver rifle. It was light as a feather and as he turned it over in his hands, he couldn't find any means of loading the weapon.

"That's one of the new toys. Fully electronic. Fires a burst of energy that would take the head of pretty much anything, anything but the things waiting out here," one of the guards spoke, and for a moment Matt thought he was joking, but there was a look in his eyes that told a different story.

It was a short scramble down the remaining slope of the mountain, yet they were drenched in sweat nonetheless. The heat and humidity were worse than anything any of the men had felt before. Even the guards seemed to be suffering.

The ground beneath them was soft, pulling at them, making every step harder work than it needed to be.

Something about the place made Matt feel uneasy, nervous and on edge. Something scuttled along the rocks behind him. He spun around but was not in time to see anything. He shuddered and turned back to the group. To his left, one of the guards wore a similar expression. He too had jumped at the sound. For a moment their eyes met, and Matt saw fear looking back at him.

"We need to keep on the path. Don't get separated. The first hunting sport is about three miles from here. Easy terrain, no threats showing on the scanner, but ..." The lead guard caught himself when he remembered that they now had company with them.

"But what?" Levi asked. He had a waver to his voice that gave away how uneasy he felt.

They didn't need to wait for an answer. An almighty roar rang out around them. It bounced through the trees and made the ground shake, as if a passenger jet flying low overhead.

The route through the trees was an easy one; it was simple to see where the pathway had been cleared. The jungle was rich with vegetation; ferns with leaves as tall as a man, and stems as thick as an adult arm lined the path where they walked. Along the way, tall rotting piles of vegetation showed the amount of work it had taken to clear the area.

The arrowhead formation of the guards was an effective setup. The three men were in the middle, Levi and Wallace together as always, and Matt took up the rear.

The temperature within the trees was muggy and wet, moisture hung in the air like a mist, and steam rose from the wetter sections of ground. While the path had been cleared, the muddy ground compacted and flattened through repeated use, but it still did not make for easy walking. The military-style boots they wore and the heavy packs they carried were already taking their toll on the three men, and they had not yet walked two miles.

The deeper they moved, the more the jungle came to life around them. The sounds of insects and wildlife scurrying through the undergrowth became more common, and above their heads, the trees rustled as birds and other animals moved through the tree tops, jumping from on to another with ease.

"The first two hunting platforms are up ahead. It is split into two. We have one spot up in the trees, and another about two hundred yards further up. Ambrose, Finn, you take the good doctor here and move through to the ground level spot. Hughes, Cipollini and I will take the others up the trees," the lead guard instructed, never once letting go of his rifle.

"What are we going to see?" Matt asked. There was something off about everything, and Matt wanted to be prepared for whatever waited for them.

"You will see the biggest game of your life. Just remember the rules. Nobody fires before I give the command. You get one kill each, and then we move on to the next zone. Do I make myself clear?" The guard spoke to them as if they were soldiers.

"Well, I'm not going to be killing anything, so if one of you two want my_" Matt began but was cut off by laughter from the guards.

"What do you mean you're not going to kill? We are out here so you can hunt big game. What else do you plan on doing, just watching the things?" The lead guard seemed genuinely confused by Matt's attitude.

"I didn't come here to hunt." Matt stood his ground.

"Okay, alright. It's your two hundred grand not mine," he sneered.

"Stop being such a damned embarrassment, boy," Wallace snapped. "I paid good money to bring you here, and god damn it, you will appreciate it."His face darkened like the sky in an approaching storm. The purple colouration of his nose seemed to light up, the red veins under his skin glowing also.

"Dad, calm down, remember …" Levi stepped between father and son, and while what he said was inaudible, it clearly worked because Wallace calmed down and took a step back.

"Fine, do what you want," he spat.

The group split into two and they set off. Matt was pleased for the chance to break away from his family, and found his pace quickening.

"You and your family don't get on, do you?" Either Ambrose or Finn asked once they were out of earshot of the other group.

"Is it that obvious?" Matt answered. He had no argument with the guards. They clearly feared the world they were in, and keeping the hunters safe was their responsibility. However, he was not in the mood to rehash family history with them.

"Well, whatever it was, I'm not sure my family would fork out two hundred grand on me in one shot like that, and I'm the fucking favourite kid," the other one of either Ambrose or Finn added as they walked.

Neither man had a South African accent. Matt wasn't sure why that dawned on him so powerfully, or why he even considered it important.

"What is this place?" he asked as he wiped the sweat from his brow.

"You're about to find out," Finn or Ambrose answered. "The lookout spot is right through here. You will need to get down low and crawl a way, maybe fifteen or twenty yards. Something like that." The instructions came in a well-rehearsed manner, like a flight attendant going through the safety instructions.

"Remember, do not discharge your weapon until you hear the signal from Captain Howard, do you understand?" the taller of the guards spoke. His face was strong and his jaw large and angular. It was clear that beneath the uniform, he was nothing but muscle. The other guard was softer, and carried a quieter demeanour.

"How am I supposed to hear him?" Matt asked.

"Through the communicator, here," the softer of the two answered. He stepped forward and opened Matt's pack. He pulled out a small radio transmitter, which he fixed onto Matt's jacket. The earpiece slid around his ear, and instantly he was back in touch with the others. He could hear Captain Howard giving the same instructions to his father and brother.

"Good luck, and whether you kill anything or not, keep your weapon ready. Take your time and remember, wait for the signal." The harder man, who stuck Matt as more of a Finn than an Ambrose, slapped him on the shoulder.

The large ferns that lined the path were thick and untouched by the workers. Their towering stems and long leaves were heavy, and Matt needed both hands to move them out of the way. Dropping to his knees, Matt crawled through the mud. Beneath the plants, the steam had no way to escape. The ground was soft and wet and felt as if it were sucking him down into it. There was a strong, peaty odour to the jungle once you got close enough to it. Not a horrid smell, but one that was noticeable nonetheless.

Matt was out of breath and panting by the time he pulled himself free of the trees. He had only stopped once when something rustled beside him. It had moved fast, but a moment of fear had frozen him. He envisioned a scorpion or some other jungle creature striking out at him. Who knew what lay in wait amidst the jungle leaves. He had watched enough nature documentaries to have an idea, and it was one he did not want to think about.

The lookout spot had been cleared in similar fashion to the pathway through the trees. The ground had been compacted flat, the ferns and plants were piled up heaps of wet rotting vegetation at the rear of the lookout.

Two long troughs had been dug into the ground, space enough for a man to fit in each, bringing them down even lower, giving them a better view of proceedings.

Getting into position, Matt took a moment to catch his breath before he allowed the surroundings to take it away again.

The jungle continued for another twenty or thirty yards before it stopped and gave way to a large clearing. In the background, rising above the trees, were mountains. Their faces were black as onyx. A river twinkled in the sun as it snaked its way down their rocky face. Drawing his eyes back to the clearing, Matt saw water glinting in the middle, a pool. He knew without looking that it was fed by the river he could see in the background.

Tall grasses and large wild flowers the size of dinner plates grew in random clusters and in all manner of colours.

Moving his weapon into position, Matt fell behind the scope and used it to take a closer look at the world. It was stunning without the larger wildlife they had come to see. He knew his father and brother were missing the point, seeing through the beauty. He could hear Wallace's grumbling through his ear, but happily drowned it out.

Matt watched as insects buzzed around the flowers. It took a few moments for him to realize that the size of the flowers and the size of the insects was beyond unusual. The creatures he saw were the size of crows, but had the same striped markings as wasps. A long stinger extended several inches from their body and had a distinctive curl to the tip.

Looking at the scene with his own eyes, Matt knew something was wrong with the world. It was not one where they belonged.

Alarms sounded in his head, thoughts pulled straight and an image formed, but not clear enough for him to understand what it was showing him.

"Hold your fire. Wait for the signal," Matt heard Captain Howard growl in his ear. He couldn't help but smile at his family's ineptitude.

Something moved to his right. Matt looked across and gave a gasp as he came face to face with a cat-sized rodent. The head peering through the thick foliage. In his shock, his finger pulled the trigger of his weapon. To Matt's relief, it didn't fire. He had yet to activate the firing mechanism of his new-age weapon. He let out a long shaky breath and watched the rodent again. It sniffed the air, its cold, black eyes watching Matt. It tilted its head to one side, and after a moment of contemplation, it was gone. Scurrying back into the jungle away from the human, and the threat it possessed.

With his eyes back on the clearing, Matt alternated between the close-up view of the scope and the true panoramic experience of the naked eye.

"Look, over there," he heard Levi speak. Their vantage point giving them a better view of what was coming.

A moment later and Matt saw them also. They were the strangest creatures he had ever seen. They walked on two legs, their bodies covered in brown feathers with long tails that stretched behind them, curling up when they stood still, and uncurling when they moved. They had short, stubby beaks that ranged in colour from black to a vivid blue.

"What are they?" Matt asked, but there was nobody around to offer any explanation.

He stared at the creatures, enthralled at their appearance. They looked, to his mind at least, like a bizarre cross between a chicken and an ape; more specifically a sort of gibbon.

They ran through the grass, but stopped suddenly. They stood up straight, their eyes darting from one direction to the other. They could sense danger, and something told Matt that it was not him and his family.

"We have incoming. At your three o'clock. Three hundred yards and closing. Hold your fire. Do not make a move until we give the signal," Captain Howard spoke, his voice a mixture of fear and excitement.

Matt watched to the right. The creatures, whatever they were, moved fast, and were hidden by the tall grass. Matt only saw them when the first of their group leaped into the air, attacking the helpless chicken-like creature. They looked like lizards, only they ran on long, powerful legs. Leaning forward, their long tails whipped behind them, narrowing to a fine point at the end. Their front arms reached towards the floor, and gave them the general appearance of being off balance, as if they were somehow reaching forward to brace themselves for a fall.

Matt refused to accept what it was he saw. His mind knew, but he could not bring himself to accept it for what it was.

The lizard creature leaped through the air, and he saw two large claws unfurl, appearing from within the skin of their lower leg. The claw sliced through the chicken-thing's neck and severed its head from body in a single, swift motion. Blood spurted from the wound, jettisoning from the clean cut stump of the thing's neck.

The chicken creature stayed standing for a few moments and even managed a pace or two before it collapsed into a pool of its own blood.

The lizard creature was quick as a flash, pouncing on its downed foe, tearing strips of juicy meat from the fresh carcass. It ate with a gusto that saw it clean the meat away to the bone in just a few moments, swallowing torn mouthfuls of warm meat rather than chewing it. It would throw back its head to open up the throat, much like watching a video of a crocodile eating.

"Hold your fire," an angry voice snarled in Matt's ear. The warning went unheeded, however, for a few moments later the roar of a discharged rifle rang out. The lizard creature looked up from its meal and a moment later its head exploded from the impact of the .375 calibre round. Shattered bone and steaming chunks of flesh and brain flew in all directions. Blood misted the air. The creature's tongue remained attached, and flapped uselessly on the meaty stalk that had been its throat. The blast had curled the flesh of the creature's neck backwards like a peeled banana. The creature remained standing, even without a head. A second warning came through the earpiece just before a second blast tore a hole in its flank, blasting a fist-sized hole between the ribs. Blood poured from the wound which stretched as the path of the bullet tore open its belly, spilling long strands of steaming intestines to the floor.

"You fools!" Matt heard the booming voice of Captain Howard. "Fall back. Fall back." He gave the order, his voice filled with panic.

A high-pitched wail echoed around the clearing as the other members of the pack, which was the only word Matt thought appropriate to describe their collective, turned their attention towards the hunters.

"We need to move. Now," Ambrose called, his voice not coming through the headset but from behind him. Matt jumped when the hand landed on his shoulder and pulled him away.

They crawled through the ferns as fast as they could. Freezing when a burst from an M16 rang out. Somebody screamed. It was impossible to tell who, because it was a cry that defied description. More gunfire followed and by the time Matt and Ambrose made it out of the plants and to their feet, the bodies of three more creatures lay panting on the floor. Bullets had peppered their flesh turning their bodies into leaking masses of meat. The creatures shuddered and groaned as their lives slipped away on the rivulets of blood from their many wounds.

"There are still two more …" Captain Howard began, but the creatures pounced. They appeared from nowhere, one coming from either side of the path.

Captain Howard reacted fast, jumping to one side as the first creature snapped its hungry jaws in his direction. Acting on instinct, he raised his booted foot and kicked the creature on the jaw. Stunning it, he unsheathed the knife from his belt and drove it into the lizard's neck. Twisting the blade, he opened up the vein and blood gusted from the wound as if it were a faucet.

The second one struck from the right. Its jaws closed and bit Howard's arm clean from his body. Howard roared and fell to the floor, the bloody stump that extended a few inches below his shoulder haemorrhaged blood so fast Matt could see the man grow paler by the second.

The roar of three M16s rang out in stereo as the three remaining guards opened fire, filling the creature's body with enough lead to sink an elephant. The stream of bullets nearly severed its neck from the rear, exposing the bones of its neck. The weight of the skull caused the head to fall forward, further tearing the wound and sending a fresh shower of blood spurting into the air. Levi, who had been standing not far from the creature, caught the brunt of the shower and fell to the floor retching from the mouthful of blood he had swallowed.

"Those things … what are those things?" Wallace stuttered. He held his hunting rifle, but had not made any attempt to fire it or come to assistance.

"They are dinosaurs," Matt answered unintentionally. He needed to say it, to hear his voice pronounce the words.

"Yes, Troodons if you must know," Ambrose answered. He looked shaken, his skin pale and pasty.

"How do you know?" Matt asked.

"It's a simple biometric scan …" Ambrose began. He shook his wrist to indicate the watch he was referring to.

A cry of pain broke their strained conversation. Captain Howard had pulled himself into a seated position, his arm raining steaming drops of blood onto the jungle floor. His face was white and his jaw clenched shut. He was already growing pale from the blood loss and the sweat that slicked his brow was clearly different to the heat-driven sweat from earlier.

"We need to get back to the Spider. There has been a breach somewhere," the guard whose name Matt did not know spoke. A younger man, clearly the youngest of the group. He was covered in blood, and that was when Matt thought about the first scream, the first guard to die.

"Can we move him?" Ambrose asked.

"Yes," Matt interrupted, stepping passed them all, he crouched down to look at the wound. "We have to act fast, because it will get infected." He made it a point to stress the certainty of his statement. "But if we can wrap it up tight, we can stem the bleeding long enough for us to get back to the Spider." Matt looked at the other guards. He could not stomach to look at his own family.

"It's a long way back," Levi chipped in. "I mean, let's be realistic here. These predators can smell blood–" He stopped talking when the nameless guard held his hunting knife against his throat and backed him up against a tree.

"It is your fault that this happened. Follow the orders. They were simple. This whole place was crafted to give you all a nice time, a couple of quick kills, and then out again. But now, every creature in this world would have heard that fire fight," the man snarled.

"Cipollini, back off. We don't have time. We need to get him patched up, and us out of here." Ambrose moved towards the pair, who remained standing where they were.

"That's enough from all of you," Captain Howard barked and then fell into a coughing fit that rendered his defiance moot.

Matt ignored the quarrel going on behind him. His family posed a threat to the group, but he trusted the guards to do what was necessary. He worked quickly to bandage the wound. The first three layers of bandages he applied were soaked through with blood before he had finished wrapping. After he applied the seventh layer, he was convinced the blood flow had been stemmed, for the time being, at least.

"Can you walk?" Matt asked the Captain.

"Yes," he grunted. It was a lie, and they both knew it.

"Help me get him up," Matt spoke to Ambrose, who had crouched down beside him.

Finn and Cipollini had taken a guarded position on either side of the group, their bodies moving from left to right, and back again; a constant swivel as they searched for any sign of an attack.

The walk back to the Spider was a slow one, and the jungle felt as if it were closing in on them with every step they took.

Matt and Ambrose walked on either side of the injured captain. The wound still bled, and the first spots of red had started to stain the bandages. The man was shivering while sweat poured from him as if he stood under a shower.

The end of the treeline was in sight, the mountain that housed the Spider unit could be seen in the distance. Ambrose grunted under the strain of carrying his captain, who offered very little in the way of assistance in walking, but for the rest, the group was silent.

Their hopes died, however, when the light of the jungle's exit was blocked, and the bone-jarring roar of prehistoric death barrelled their way.

CHAPTER 6

Julian and Tracy were alone in the underground lab. Since the departure of the first tourist group, things had gone back to a semblance of normal. They were left largely to their own devices.

The personnel that had been enlisted to aid in the building of whatever it was they had built in the other world had been taken care of. None had made it back through the Spider, and both scientists knew better than to make any inquisitions as to their fate.

Albert came by every now and then, but for the most part his visits were short and almost sweet. He would wheel himself in, flanked as always by his two bodyguards, enquire about the welfare of his group, and then leave.

Life was almost simple again.

Tracy was busy working on one of the machines, adjusting the settings that ensured the Spider remained active but not too much of a drain on the power grid. She was engrossed in her work. Julian knew because she was biting her lower lip, a subconscious tick she had whenever she was fully absorbed by a task.

"I love you," Julian spoke out of the blue, as he walked across to her. Sliding his arms between hers and her body, he pulled her into an embrace and kissed her neck.

"I'm sorry, what?" Tracy asked and Julian laughed.

"Are you asking because you didn't hear me or because you can't believe what I said?" He smiled. Spinning her around, he kissed her deeply.

"Definitely the first one," she said with a smile, wrapping her arms around his neck.

"I said I love you." Julian smiled as the look of shock came over her face.

"I really should have heard that the first time." Tracy looked stunned, and a little guilty.

"That is exactly why I love you." Julian leaned in close for another kiss.

"I love you too," Tracy whispered.

Their embrace was ended shortly after when two alarms began to sound on the Spider's main console.

"I've lost the vital signs on Private Hughes," Julian called, his mind fully focused on the task at hand once more.

"I've got elevated readings on everybody in the ground." Tracy and Julian turned to look at one another. "Something has gone wrong out there," she spoke, reading the thoughts from Julian's mind as they formed.

"Problems?" Albert's sneering, snake-like voice hissed through the lab.

"Now is not the time, Mr. Wilhelm," Julian answered, catching his tone and adding the formality to the end as a means of tempering his reaction.

"I see that. Keep me informed." Albert did not seem in the least bit concerned about the welfare of anybody in the party, and simply turned and left the room.

While the sirens blared and the lab sounded as if it were under attack in some way or another, there was very little that either Julian or Tracy could do. Their job was to monitor and report, beyond that, they could offer no support or service to those that had travelled through the Spider.

They silenced the alarms and stood quietly as the screen for Private Hughes, a man neither of them knew in any form, confirmed that his life had been lost. There was no chance of a false reading, for the group were all wearing biometric trackers that were activated the minute they passed through the Spider. They were not readings from a machine, but reading straight from the body itself.

The mood had changed, and as Tracy wrapped her arms around Julian, it was a different sort of comfort that she sought.

CHAPTER 7

Lead filled the air as both Finn and Cipollini opened fire on the beast. The dinosaur was the size of a bus. Its hind legs were rippling with muscle, the scaly skin stretched to the point of bursting.

It stared at them, seemingly ignoring the bullets that tore into its flesh. With another roar, it charged them down. The ground trembled with each thudding step the beast took. The guards held their position, their attention directed away from the creature's body up towards its head.

A burst of fire tore through the creature's eyes, bursting them like grapes. White fluid, stained pink with blood, oozed from the sockets. Sightless, the creature roared once more, only it was now a cry of pain. Careening from its path it ran into the trees, shattering their trunks and filling the air with sap and splinters. The dinosaur ran a few more yards, before it collapsed into a heap, its giant frame shuddering as it struggled to hold onto life.

"We should put it out of its misery," Matt spoke when he saw that the creature was far from dead.

"Then you do it, son. Go on, shoot that bitch," Wallace spoke with a laugh. Matt turned to face him. He could not believe what he was hearing. "Yeah, I thought as much. Come on, boy. Let's get out of here. I want my damned money back for sure," Wallace growled.

"I wouldn't walk that way if I were you," Ambrose spoke softly. He could see the way the old man treated his sons. From the short time he had spent with Matt, he liked the doctor, and his dislike for the father was instant.

"Why not, soldier boy? That is the way out, isn't it?" Wallace growled. He was shaken by the experience, but would be damned if he let anybody know.

"Well for a start, we should move as a unit." Finn stepped forward to add his part into the conversation.

"And also, those things, the albertosaurus," Ambrose pointed at the shuddering dinosaur with his free arm, "they move in pairs, one male and one female." Ambrose words fell silent as a growl rolled through the trees like thunder.

The beast appeared from within the trees, the head peering through the trunks, checking to make sure the disturbance was worth fighting over. Raising its large, scaled snout into the air it sniffed. The scent of blood, death, and gun smoke was heavy.

"Run!" Wallace cried out, and he and Levi turned and fled from the group, running deeper into the jungle.

"Stop, you fools," Cipollini called after them. "You will only draw–"

Behind him, the creature stepped from the trees.

The dinosaur was larger than the nearly expired male, but clearly from the same breed. A strip of red scales ran through the middle of her head, blending into the brownish-green colour that was the rest of its body.

It took a step, cautious at first, but it soon took another, and another, the pace quickening until it was charging at a run. The remaining men had no choice but to turn and flee after Wallace and Levi, who had disappeared from view, swallowed by the jungle. Finn took the lead, with Matt behind him, still clutching his high-powered, ultra-modern rifle, still unable to bring himself to even consider firing it. Behind Matt, Ambrose limped as fast as he could manage, lugging his captain along with him. Cipollini brought up the rear, firing repeated small bursts at the creature. It seemed that in its rage, pain was a factor that was no longer recognized.

"Leave me," Captain Howard gasped.

Their pace had slowed as Ambrose struggled to haul the as-good-as-dead weight of his captain at any noteworthy speed.

"Never, sir," Ambrose answered.

"That's an order, Private. Let me go. I'm done for anyway. I can't go on with just one arm in a place like this. Run, save yourself now." With the dwindling strength he had, Howard pushed the young private Ambrose away from him, creating the separation he needed.

His bloody knife lay on the floor where he had dropped it after losing his arm. He turned to face the creature as Cipollini ran towards him.

"Get out of here," Howard yelled in a final surge of defiance.

He turned to face the charging female albertosaurus and held the knife he had stolen from Cipollini out towards her.

"Come on, you bitch," he snarled.

The dinosaur didn't even slow its pace as it neared the man. Jaws opened and snapped shut. Howard waited and threw himself to his knees. He felt the rush of air as the jaws snapped shut above his head. Raising his knife, he thrust it into the belly of the creature.

The female albertosaurus ran over the captain, chasing the rest of the group. The serrated blade cut through the underside of the dinosaur, drowning him in a waterfall of blood and gore. Long, thick strands of intestines fell from the gaping wound, which extended the length of the body. With the intestines gone, large organs also fell from her belly until the creature was nothing but a hollow shell of the beast she was. The dinosaur stopped its run and opened her mouth to roar, but nothing came out. The giant frame crashed to the jungle floor, the throes of death already reaching their peak. It still died before its male mate.

Behind it, lost in the sea of offal, lay Captain Howard. His body lay twisted and broken, blood and guts covered every inch of his body.

"We can't stop. We need to keep moving." Ambrose pulled on Matt's shoulder. The two were the only ones who had stood to witness the act that undoubtedly saved their lives.

They caught up with the others a while later. Their tracks had been easy to follow, but their pace frantic. Moving deeper into the jungle was not an idea that Matt liked, or was in favour of, but he was not going to go it alone. Even if the Spider was not too far from where they had been, he knew that if anything else came out of the bushes to surprise him, he would not be able to defend himself.

The four men were leaning against the trunks of a group of closely clustered trees. They were exhausted. Sweat dripped from their heads, and the two guards had even ditched their heavy jackets and were down to their sweat-soaked t-shirts.

Wallace was taking deep gulps of air as he tried to force his lungs to take in more and more oxygen. He looked as if he was about to keel over and die. Matt found his eyes lingering on his father for a moment or two longer than the others, watching just in case his first thoughts were to be realized. Then there was Levi. He was covered from head to toe in blood. A steaming pile of pink-tinted vomit laid spread at his feet. He was leaned forward, his hands on his knees. Stringy strands of clotted blood hung from his hair, but Matt thought it better not to mention it.

"What do we do now?" Matt asked. "I guess the hunting party is over with."

"You'd fucking love that wouldn't you, boy? Oh great, we can just go home now," Wallace snapped, shoving his right hand into his trouser pocket.

"What do you want us to do, *Dad?*" The emphasis used on the parental word made it clear to everybody that it was not being used as a term of endearment.

"I paid good money to come out here to kill a fucking dinosaur." In his exhaustion, he almost sounded drunk. His words sloshed together, and he swayed on his feet.

"Fuck that for a game of soldiers, Dad. I just want to get out of here," Levi spoke, lifting his head, craning his neck while the rest of his body stayed still, to look at his old man.

Rage flashed in Wallace's eyes. An anger and hatred that Matt recognized instantly.

"There is no room for debate. The safari is cancelled, we are getting out of here," Finn stepped forward and spoke. Out of the three guards, he seemed to be the one holding up the best. Wallace moved to interrupt him, but the strong-jawed guard was one step ahead of him. "Oh, you will get to kill your dinosaur alright, old man. No more hunting spots. It is open fucking season and you get to take home the prize." There was a no-nonsense tone to Finn's voice that even Wallace didn't argue with.

"So, we just head back to the Spider thing and sleep in real beds tonight?" Levi asked.

"No," Finn answered, turning on them. Ambrose jumped up too, intercepting Finn's full response, knowing that he had the better people skills out of the two.

"We can't go back just yet. The gunfire would have attracted too much attention, not to mention the scent of blood in the air. No, we need to move away from this place, and then double back. The safari moves in a circuit. We cleared the pathway ourselves, well, not us, but you know what I mean." His gaze fell on Matt, who stood between his father and brother, who were leaning against trees on opposite sides of the path.

"How long will it take?" Matt wanted to know, understanding that Ambrose wanted the conversation to be between them, and them alone.

"If we can keep moving, and not run into any trouble, we should be back at the Spider in three days. We have enough ammo to survive. Each station is filled with it, along with some basic rations. We have a good-sized team, and if we all work together then we can get through this. I know we can."

"Then what do you suggest is our first move?" Matt asked, and Wallace gave a loud grunt of disapproval.

"That's my boy. The great and fearless fucking sheep. I don't know where I went wrong with you," the familiar tirade began.

"Shut up," Matt snapped, and a look of shock crossed the old man's face.

"I don't like you," Finn, who was standing closer to Wallace, growled. "I've dealt with lots of people like you over the years, and trust me when I say that if anything goes wrong, you will die first." He spoke through clenched teeth, even his jaw seemed to ripple with muscle. "Why?" he asked. "I will tell you why. Because nobody here will risk their life to save you." The venom in the words was pure as the driven snow. With his message given, and Wallace cowered ever so slightly, Finn moved out and led them into the jungle.

The walk to the area that had been cleared as a camp site was uneventful. The worst thing any of them encountered was blisters on their feet from the boots. Wallace kept his mouth shut, moving with his head down, and a limp that grew more pronounced the further they walked.

While they encountered nothing, there were plenty of growls and calls carried on the air that ensured they never forgot where they were. The occasional crash of a tree nearby never failed to add an extra skip into their step either.

"We will make our camp here. The nights fall quickly in this place, and we want to make sure that we are settled before the darkness falls. That is when this world really comes to life," Ambrose addressed the group as they stopped.

Levi looked around, the path they followed looked no different here than at any other point. "Why here?" he asked with genuine confusion.

"Oh, I don't mean on the ground. God no, we wouldn't survive the first few hours. No, we make camp up there." Ambrose pointed high into the trees where three large platforms had been erected, lashed to the branches.

"How do you expect us to get up there?" Wallace growled, his anger anything but dissipated by their trek.

"We have a system rigged—" Ambrose began.

"But I think you can fucking climb them," Finn interrupted, making no attempt to hide his dislike.

Wallace swallowed hard and stepped back. Even he knew that authority was not only decided by rank, and he had no option but to concede.

They made their camp in the trees, at least fifty feet from the floor. The platform that had been created was solid. Much more so than it looked. It moved in a circle, like a donut. The base was fifteen feet wide, and moved through the trees leaving a hollow center maybe five meters in diameter. Each man carried a tent with them, and none had lost their packs in the skirmishes. Matt waited, watching as his father and brother erected their tents. Together, but with a distance between them that he had not expected.

Once they were settled, he moved across the platform to where Ambrose had pitched his tent, he too seeking distance from the others. Matt paused before he made his camp. There was plenty of room for him to move elsewhere if the guard insisted upon his solitude.

"It's fine. You can pitch your tent here," the guard replied.

Matt made his tent and got settled, surprised at how comfortable he found the things he carried, and how little the situation, or the trees bothered him. The years in the ER had steeled his nerves when it came to stressful situations. While he had never considered the way a dinosaur attack would impact him, it was clear to see that mentally, preparation was key.

Sitting on the platform, leaning against his still-rolled up sleeping bag, Matt watched the others. His father was sitting inside his tent, hiding away. Every now and then he would emerge, but in the time Matt watched, the time it took for the sun to set and twilight to reign, Wallace had crept back into his tent seven times.

Levi moved slower, his body still red with dried blood. It was clearing slowly, the dried, rusted flakes of dinosaur gore chipped away like old paint.

Finn was moving around, his rifle still in his hands. His tent was made and he had set to building a fire in a pit that had been built into the platform. Cipollini followed Finn, and from a distance Matt saw it for what it was. Cipollini, the young and impressionable novice was desperate for approval, following the lead not of his captain, but of the strongest member of the group. The physical specimen and undoubted alpha male. Once realized, it was quite comical.

"You and your family? What's the deal there?" Ambrose asked as he sat down beside Matt. They looked, the whole group, like nothing more than friends on a retreat. The dangers of the lost world they were stranded in were forgotten. "If you don't mind me asking," he added quickly.

"It's a long story," Matt answered.

"It's going to be a long night." Ambrose smiled.

"My family is a difficult thing to explain. At least, I thought it was. The years have shown me that I was wrong. We are far more typical than even I want to believe. My father was abusive, and there is no doubt in my mind that he still is. My mother escaped with me, but my brother there, he was always a daddy's boy, and nothing would change his mind." Matt found the words came easily to him. The family history was not something he liked to think about too often.

"Sounds like a familiar tale," Ambrose said, nodding. "I always told myself, I would never drink a drop, after my old man broke my arm on Christmas. My mother never left him, well, not until the good Lord came to rescued her himself. You got any kids?" Ambrose asked.

"No," Matt answered.

"I've got three. Two girls and a boy. Check this out." He spoke the way any father should speak about his children, with a beaming pride that shone through his every pore. He pulled a crumpled photo out of his bag. It was of his wife and kids. His wife was a beautiful woman. Hispanic, or so she seemed, with long black hair and a face that was as cute as it was attractive. The kids, luckily, had taken after their mother in the looks' department.

"They are beautiful, man." Matt nodded, as he watched the photograph. "What brings you out here?"

"The money. I didn't know what I was getting into when I came. I answered a call about personal security. That Wilhelm guy, he is a liar and a tyrant. He keeps us locked inside in the other world. One wrong move and he would kill you where you stood." Ambrose sniffed, a cover to hide the tears at the fresh thoughts of his children. "I've not seen them in almost three months," he added, the words ripe with pain.

On the other side of the platform, the fire was going. It was only small but it ate greedily at the sticks it was fed.

"What brings you out here then?" Ambrose asked. "If you did not want to hunt, why come? This trip isn't cheap." He pushed through curiosity rather than for any ulterior motives.

"The price is something else entirely. I have no idea how he got the money for it. As for why, my mother died, and he sold me a line while I was mourning. He promised me to my face that we would not be hunting. I should have known better." Matt thought back to the night in the bar. He had known then his father was lying. Deep down, he had known.

"Can't pick your family, hey," Ambrose offered, understanding the pain Matt felt.

"Amen to that," Matt answered. "Hey, I've been meaning to ask. Back there, how did you know what sort of dinosaurs they were? Are you some kind of palaeontologist or something, on the side?"

"Nah man, I loved 'em as a kid, but I'm no expert. We have these watches, look." Ambrose held up his arm and pulled at his sleeve. He was wearing a large square watch. It looked, for all intents and purposes, like any other watch you would see in the store. "This thing can scan the area and tells us what the dinosaur is. It works for most creatures, and in one-on-one situations, it seems to be pretty good. In groups, not so much." Ambrose's voice trailed away.

"Groups?"

"Yeah, a few months ago we got caught by a group of dinos. They were fighting over territory, didn't even notice us. We lost four men that day. I've never heard people make such a noise as old Rusev did. He was the biggest man I have ever seen and when they bit him in half, he just refused to die. He crawled and crawled. If the triceratops hadn't stamped on his head, I have no doubt that he would still be out there, crawling towards safety."

"You lost a lot of people setting this up?" Matt asked.

"A few. The building crews. They lost a lot."

"Why?"

"The dinosaurs."

"No, I mean why do you do this, here, in this world? What is the end game?" Matt wanted to understand.

"Mr. Wilhelm, he recruited us all. He is a very rich man, with very big connections. It's all about money. He learned about the Spider technology, and then bought the program. That way nobody could stop him. I'm just a grunt in all of this. But there is always talk, you know, through the grapevine." Ambrose seemed relaxed, and Matt had no reason not to believe him.

There were plenty of other questions he had. Some he hoped Ambrose could answer, and others he needed to ask simply to clear them from his mind. There was no time for further talk, however, for moments later, their camp was infiltrated. Two bird-like creatures part-fluttered, part-clumsily fell from the trees above them. They were the size of large chickens, but with a long, peacock-style tail that extended behind them, effectively doubling their length. Their torso was covered in what looked like fur, a reflective, rich and gorgeous blue. The large wings, which they tucked awkwardly against their body, were feathered. Along the upper portion, they were the same blue as their torso, but as you moved towards the tips, the feathers paled to an icy blue that gave them an electric appearance.

The creatures stood and stared around them, studying the platform. They appeared confused as to where they were. They made a primitive clucking sound, something akin to that of a turkey. They watched the two men, who were watching them in return. Their heads tilted to one side for a moment, and then they fell to the floor with a shower of blood.

Their bodies twitched and wings fluttered as they succumbed to the cerebral separation. Loose feathers were shaken free by the quiver of death's touch and fell into the gathering pool of blood.

Finn stood behind the dead birds, his hunting knife in hand. He had removed his jacket and stood shirtless. His tattooed skin was bulging with muscle, so much so that it looked stretched taut over his frame.

"Looks like we can eat fresh meat tonight." He spat onto the platform and gave a laugh. Finn grabbed the birds by the tail, and dragged them after him as he moved towards the fire. He left a long, bloody smear in his wake.

Matt watched the man, and deep down something stirred inside him, some deep hidden part of him admired the way he dealt out death so swiftly and without any visible remorse. He and Finn were much alike as a result of their differences. Both dealt with death, and acted without thinking, trusting their instincts. The only different was that one's nature was to take the lives that came its way, while the other chose to save them.

Matt sat back and watched, thoughtful as a rivulet of blood flowed towards the edge of the platform, pausing before falling to the jungle floor. An electric blue feather was carried on the crimson tide. It was stained red, ruined forever. Matt watched it fall, the weight of the blood even removed the grace of its final descent.

"If you want to eat, you had better come get a piece," Finn called across, uncaring about his voice drawing more unwarranted attention.

"That guy is tough as nails, but as dumb as they come," Ambrose commented. "Still, some real meat would go down well." Ambrose got up and moved towards the fire.

Finn had moved fast, skinning the birds and eviscerating them. A steaming pile of guts lay on the platform not far from the fire.

Matt followed Ambrose, his stomach growling at the smell of the meat, but his eyes could not leave the pile of guts.

"Good god, grow a pair, boy," Wallace growled. "It's just a pile of guts." He slurred as he spoke and swayed as he moved to sit down, half-falling the last bit. He let out a belch and the familiar stench of rum was heavy on his breath.

"You've been drinking." Matt looked at him incredulously.

"I think after today a drink is deserved, don't you?" he snapped.

"You're a drunk, stop making excuses." Matt felt the last strand of his patience snap. "It was you that couldn't listen. You that fired the shots that caused all the trouble we are in. You are a useless, selfish asshole of a man." Matt felt the rage surge through him, spilling over in an all-consuming wave.

"I might be a drunk, but you are an ungrateful brat. A worthless accident that I never wanted. Your dearly departed mother tricked me into having you. I regret the day you ever slid out of her cunt," Wallace shouted, trying to get to his feet. He was stopped when a fist collided with his jaw. Wallace was sent sprawling to the floor, and it took the quick reaction of Finn to catch the old man before he stumbled from the platform.

"That's my brother you are talking about," Levi growled. He stood with his shoulders tensed. "If it wasn't for you, we would–" Levi cried deep, shuddering sobs. His face was still caked with blood, and his eyes were wide and wild.

"That's enough," Finn growled. "We don't have time for your family squabbles. Sit the hell down and let's eat some bird." He looked over at Wallace, who had managed to drag himself back into a sitting position. "Drink what the hell you like, but you get into problems, I will leave your drunk ass behind in a second." His eyes seemed to bulge from his head as he turned up the intensity of his stare.

Wallace paid it no mind, instead, he reached forward and tore a leg from one of the birds that was roasting on a makeshift spit above the fire. He bit into the limb. The sound of the crisp skin and the initial pop of the moist meat beneath was too much for them all, and they descended, Matt included, on the meat.

As they ate, Matt watched his brother. In all of the years, Levi had never physically stood up for his brother. He watched him, thankful, relieved that he had finally seen sense. There was a look to his eyes, however, that told a far more disturbing story.

Levi sat hunched over, holding his meat with two hands. He ate slowly and thoughtfully. Eating on instinct rather than anything on a more conscious level. His eyes were dull, and he stared into nothing, lost in thought. Only Matt knew the thoughts that were swirling round his brother's mind, and he just hoped that it was not too late for him to fight back against them.

After the altercation with Wallace, who remained on his best behaviour while they ate, but promptly fell into a drunken doze not long after, the mood in the group was subdued. The birds had tasted good. Meaty and filling. But their aroma had attracted other unwarranted attention.

At some point in the night, once the darkness around them had become near total, Finn, at least Matt assumed it was Finn, kicked the pile of cold dinosaur guts from the edge of the platform. They landed with a wet splat on the jungle floor. A few moments later came the frantic snarls and grunts of creatures fighting for the tasty morsels that had fallen from the heavens.

The guards set up a watch, with Cipollini taking the first shift. When Ambrose retired, Matt took the opportunity to follow him.

Sleep did not come easy. Especially with the sounds of the lost jungle and the beasts that dwelled within it echoing around the camp. Matt tried not to focus on the different growls and howls, but it was impossible not to.

Sleep came eventually, but it was restless and far from easy. In his dream, he was back in the hunting spot with his father. He was a boy again, and his father was berating him for not wanting to take the shot.

"Look through the scope, boy, and pull the trigger," Wallace roared, his voice echoed like artillery fire.

Doing as he was told, Matt looked through the scope. The setting was the same, but the deer was gone. In its place stood a dinosaur. It was a strange-looking creature, tall on several levels. Long thin legs, with a pair of bulging knuckles on each which gave way to a tall oddly-coloured body that seemed too wide for the narrow set of the limbs that supported it. Rising from the body was a long thick neck that finally became a comically small head. A long beak, like that of a pelican, extended from the small head, covering almost the same length as the neck itself. The creature took a step forward, and Matt saw wing-like webbing extending from the front legs, attaching to the underside of the body.

It was a peaceful-looking creature.

"Shoot it," Wallace urged. His voice was unusually soft, and seemed to echo around the secluded hunting spot. "Shoot it, shoot it, shoot it." It became a chant, a never-ending loop that seeped through Matt's head and made it ache.

The words created a wind that swept around him, whipping sand and dust until it was all Matt could see. He still held the rifle, his finger curled around the trigger. The storm cleared, the dust fell, and the creature was gone. In its place was his father. A giant, swollen image of his father, stretched to the size of a deer. Long bloody antlers extended from his head, strands of bloody guts and offal were strung between them.

Matt tightened his grip on the gun, and adjusted his eyes behind the scope. His finger caressed the trigger, pulling it just a little, not enough to discharge the weapon, but enough to make him feel the potential energy of the round as it sat in the chamber.

The twisted image of his father jolted upright, as it if had heard the sound of the rifle preparing to fire. Its eyes locked on Matt and began to burn. Bright orange fire replaced the black sightless orbs that had been set into its face. It gave a roar and charged at Matt, its head lowered. The gore-covered antlers had been filed to sharp points on each spike. The ground trembled. The beast moved fast, covering the ground in an instant. Everything went black, and then Matt pulled the trigger. The sound of the shot rang out, booming like cannon fire, and suddenly Matt was awake.

He sat upright in his sleeping bag. Sweat covered every inch of his body, a foul smelling, fear-induced sweat. It hung in the sealed tent and was choking. Matt had to get out. Scrambling from the sleeping bag, he unzipped his tent and fell out onto the base of the platform. He lay there for a few moments, breathing deeply, trying to calm his trembling hand.

The jungle was warm, but compared to the heat of both the day and the tent Matt had escaped from, the air felt remarkably cool.

He got to his feet. A new day was dawning, the first few strands of light beginning to caress the jungle.

For a moment, it was a peaceful place, until the sound of a tree being felled with a single crunching blow rang out. Something gave a grunt. It came from the other side of the platform. The large circular construction was empty for the most part, with their tents focussing on two small areas, both within the first half of the platform's total area.

Moving around his tent, careful not to make any noise, Matt went for a stroll. The platform was solid, but knowing a single slip could see him plummet to the ground was enough to make every step the result of a double-thought process.

There was another crash and a series of grunts came from below the platform, and for the first time, Matt felt it sway and move.

Holding onto the tree as best he could, Matt leaned forward and peered over the edge. He could make out a shape in the pre-dawn light, but it was not something his eyes could define to any degree of accuracy. Mainly for the fact that he had never seen a creature like it. The closest approximation would be that of a moose. Only this creature was easily twice the size of any moose Matt had seen. Its antlers created a jagged bowl easily two meters across. It was rubbing its antlers against the tree, shaking its head from side to side. The impact was enough to shake both the tree and the platform.

As he watched, another creature moved into view. It was smaller than the first, but moved in from the flank. It hit the moose-like creature from the side, its antlers burying into the animal's torso. The creature threw up its head and howled, a combination of pain and anger. The smaller creature shook its head violently, and in freeing itself, also tore strips of flesh from the animal's side. The larger creature turned to face its attacker. Prepared for the second wave, it lowered its head and met the smaller foe at a charge. Their antlers collided with a heavy thud, and the smaller beast was thrown backwards from the force of the blow. One of its antlers had been ripped from its skull, caught in the intricate lacing of the alpha male's horns. Injured and unable to retreat, the beast reared up onto its hind legs and kicked out at the large male.

A snarl emanated from one of the creatures and their fight continued. Matt watched, held in stunned silence at the display being put on. He didn't notice Cipollini and Finn move closer to him.

He also didn't hear the sound their silenced rifles made as they took their shots. The head of the smaller moose creature exploded from the first wave of fire. Two rounds finding their home, one above each eye. The skull was blown open and a shower of bone shards and brain matter filled the air.

The larger creature turned around, sensing the danger. Its belly was slick with blood, and Matt knew that the gut shot it had taken would be the death of it.

It took five shots before the creature was finally put down, dying with an agonized wail.

"Why did you do that?" Matt turned to ask.

"They were a danger," Cipollini answered. "We can't be taking any risks with the creatures out here." The man smiled. "Come on, Doc, I'm just playing. They will serve as a good distraction." He pointed down to the corpse which had already caught the attention of the local predators. A group of five small dinosaurs had appeared out of nowhere. They were inspecting the felled prey. Circling them, they appeared confused until one stepped forward. It took of bite from the throat of the smaller creature, tearing away a mouthful of meat with the same crisp sound that made Matt think of eating a piece of celery.

"What sort of dinosaur are they?" Matt asked as he watched the pack descended on the bodies.

"What does it matter?" Finn answered. He walked away before Matt could offer a retort.

"Deinonychus," Ambrose answered, appearing as the two men walked away. "They are part of the raptor family, or so my watch tells me."

Matt liked Ambrose. He found himself drawn to the man, and was pleased that he had also sought his confidence the night before, talking of family and life away from the lost world.

"We need to leave. It is best to head out early with the first light," Ambrose spoke. "We have a lot of ground to cover and it was busy out there last night. We attracted a lot of attention yesterday."

Ambrose walked away and Matt followed him. He was surprised to see that his brother and father were awake. Although to look at Levi, Matt would sooner believe his brother had not been to sleep at all.

"We need to move fast." Finn gave the orders. "We have the small bastards distracted for a while, but there are some big boys out there. I could hear them in the night, and tracked their progress as best I could." He pointed back the way they had come. "Best I can tell is they moved that way, towards the mountain. I guess drawn by our fire from yesterday." Finn stopped talking and took a step back.

"If we move fast, we can make the next hunting ground within ninety minutes. We've got some real weapons there. We can arm ourselves, and get ready for the home stretch." Cipollini took over their briefing.

"What kind of weapons?" Matt asked.

"None you would use, I'm sure," Wallace growled. His eyes were swollen and red, his face screwed up into a frown.

Matt and the others ignored him. "We've got some more M16s, some grenades, knives, and a few high-powered things in case of emergency," Finn spoke proudly. Matt didn't need to ask any more to know that Finn had stocked the supplies himself.

They climbed down from the trees, Finn moving first, along with Ambrose. Matt, Levi, and Wallace followed with Cipollini bringing up the rear. They moved quietly, not wanting to disturb the deinonychus, who had already picked the first carcass clean and were working on the second.

The ground was disturbed, large footprints and deep gouges in the damp ground confirmed the activity from the night before.

It was still cool in the jungle, the sun not fully risen, but with every minute that passed, the heat built up once more.

By the time they finished their hurried walk to the hunting station, they were all sweating profusely. Their journey had been slowed by Wallace, whose condition was not optimal. His sweat stank of rum, and he had stopped three times to vomit into the bushes.

They hadn't seen any more dinosaur activity, but Matt had the uneasy feeling that they were being watched. He wanted to share his thoughts with Ambrose, but he had been separated by Finn.

The second hunting area was a hut. A construction not dissimilar to something you would see on any building site. It was a weapons store of sorts. The hunting spot itself was a few meters on the other side. The ground sloped away just beyond the trees that had been cleared, and below them another area of plains extended. There was a river that fed into a large lake in the distance, and the floor was a thick and luscious green.

There was no time to enjoy the scenery, however, as Finn and the other guards were busy tallying up their weapons cache. Matt watched as they slid long hunting knives, which looked more like serrated-edged machetes, into sheaths attached to their boots. Automatic rifles were placed over their shoulders as a reserve to the weapons they carried. Ambrose held a weapon that was different to the others. It had a secondary mechanism added to it, which had Matt puzzled at first. Then he saw the ammunition and it fell into place. It was a grenade launcher, or something with a similar purpose. Hand guns were also collected and stored on their person, just as a final measure for protection. Once they were done, guards addressed the group.

Ambrose handed Matt a double-barrelled shotgun and a belt of ammunition. He also gave him a pistol. Matt had no idea what kind, but at the end of the day it didn't matter. He slid it into the waistband of his trousers and nodded at Ambrose who turned and moved back to the others.

"I know you might not want it, but trust me, we are going to need it," he whispered to Matt as he placed the ammunition belt over his shoulders.

While the guards decided on the best course of action, Matt found himself watching his father and brother. They were locked in conversation. Wallace grew more animated with each sentence, while Levi just stood and stared at the floor. His arms were folded over one another and his head hung forward. It was a posture Matt knew well from his childhood, and he knew exactly what was being said; the threats, the disappointment, the deep-seated rage that was hurled so freely when the real Wallace came out to play.

He understood it all in that moment. His brother had not defended his father. He had been terrified of him. Matt saw it in the way Levi stood, and as images of a handful of their encounters through adulthood played out in his mind, Matt couldn't help but remember his brother's eyes. They were dead, expressionless. He was a defeated man. A man who had endured a troubled life, from childhood onwards. Matt wondered for the first time just how bad it had gotten for his brother when they had moved out. He had always thought he was the focus of his father's rage, but what if he was wrong?

Emotion surged through him, and Matt found himself striding forward. He grabbed his father by the shoulder and spun him around.

"Leave him alone," Matt growled, shoving his old man away from his brother. "You've done enough damage to our lives." There was venom in his words. A lifetime of anger and hatred that had now boiled over.

"Ungrateful bastards. Both of you. Everything I did for you, everything I taught you. Especially you." He pointed at Levi. "You need to think long and hard about this, boy. Just fucking think about it." Wallace spoke in a hushed tone, not wanting to attract the attention of the others. His face had darkened to a frightening shade of purple, and his eyes had turned black with rage.

Matt said nothing. His body had started to shake, and it took every ounce of fortitude that he had to continue looking the man in the eye.

"Leave it, Matt." Levi placed a hand on his brother's shoulder. "He's not worth it."

"You just made a big fucking mistake, kid." Wallace turned and stormed away from the hut.

"We need to stay together." Ambrose tried to stop Wallace, albeit a weak attempt.

"Fuck you, soldier boy. I can take care of myself," Wallace spat as he walked out of the building's main door. He didn't get more than a few meters before the jaws closed around him.

He gave a scream, but it was cut short as long, curled fangs punctured his chest and back, popping his lungs like balloons. Blood bubbled through his body and out of his mouth and nose. He coughed and gargled, drowning in his own visceral fluid, and then he was gone. Snatched from view at a speed that defied the human eye.

Running from the cabin, the group found themselves staring at a giant snake. The creature was easily the size of several busses laid out end to end and its head was the size of a small car. The jaw which had clenched around Wallace had dislocated itself and the creature was busy swallowing the struggling man whole. The meaty scent of blood and the foul stench of excrement filled the air from where the snake's fangs had punctured Wallace's bowel.

"No!" Levi shouted on instinct. He pulled his pistol and fired three shots at the creature. Each one found its mark and drew a strange greenish blood, but did nothing to stop the inevitable.

"Hold your fire," Finn called, but even that was too late. The snake was angered and it lashed out with a tail that caught Cipollini in the chest and sent him flying. Launched through the air, he collided with the trunk of a nearby tree. They all heard the crunching sound his spine made as the force of the blow combined with the impact bent him backwards. He fell to the floor a twitching mess. Pink foam bubbled in his mouth and his eyes rolled back into his head as the fit took hold.

"Move out," Finn roared as the snake struck again. It had swallowed Wallace and while the man's bulk could still be seen inside the enormous reptile's throat, it was clear that a second course was sought after.

The creature lunged forward, its head crashing into the metal shack with sound like a lightning strike. The wall caved in and buckled from the impact, but the giant snake was not fazed.

"We need to go down," Finn called as he came barrelling towards them, his M16 clutched in both hands. He had a look of near panic on his face, and that alone was enough to get Matt moving without question.

The only problem was that there was no clear path for them to follow and the drop to the valley below was a steep one.

"Just keep your weight on your back foot, your hand out for balance and pray to God you don't hit a tree," Ambrose said as he turned and fired a burst of his M16 into the snake's exposed underbelly. The shots were closely grouped and opened up a football-sized hole in the creature's body. Blood poured from the wound, and worst of all, Wallace's hand fell through the gash. The skin was already starting to melt away, coming off in sticky globs like candle wax, exposing the red meat beneath.

Matt looked at his brother, but there was no time to offer him any support. They jumped together and for a few moments, there was nothing beneath them. It felt as though they were suspended in the air.

Matt hit the ground and immediately felt his ankle give a sharp twist. Pain shot through his foot and up his leg, but he managed to cover the cry of pain with a determined roar as he turned his body and slid down the embankment. Finn and Ambrose were beneath him and he watched as they negotiated the slide with a dancer's grace. They reached the bottom and fluidly pulled their guns into their shoulders, ready to fire at anything that came near them.

Matt controlled his descent well enough to remain on his feet until he reached level ground. There he collapsed, his ankle screaming at him to stop. Levi arrived a few seconds later, tumbling head over heels the last few meters. He came to rest in the grass beside Matt, a nasty gash running on his forehead painted his face scarlet for the second time in as many days.

Above them, the snake had turned its attention to the cabin, as it thrashed around in pain. Every twist and turn its body made only served to further tear the whole that had been made. Everything fell silent, and while none of them could see, or cared to see it, the trickle of greenish blood that began to drip over the edge of the drop told them that the creature had not survived its encounter with man and their smoking lead.

CHAPTER 8

Matt sat up slowly. His chest felt tight and his ribs hurt like hell, but he knew enough to realize there was nothing broken, just badly bruised. His ankle was a different story. The pain from the twisted joint was a new constant, and any attempt to move sent waves of pain shooting into his brain like flares.

"Is it broken?" Levi asked.

"I don't think so." Matt stared at his foot, as if he could somehow will it to get better. "How's your head?"

"Still attached." The conversation was stilted, and the silence between them was as awkward as a badly planned first date.

"So, he's finally gone," Matt spoke before he knew it. Even after everything, he was alarmed at not only how cold the words were when he uttered them, but how unmoved he was by the fact.

"Yep." Levi had a distant look to his eyes, and Matt didn't think it was only because of the head injury.

"I'm sorry, brother," Matt began.

"Don't be. He was an asshole, and he deserved what he got." Levi spoke the words, but even Matt knew that the emotion behind them told a different story.

"I don't mean that. I mean for leaving you. I never even … never even thought he would start on you," Matt stammered, realizing how he had failed as a brother.

"That was always the problem. It was never just about you, Matt. You never understood the things I put up with just so he would leave you alone. It wasn't when you left, it was always." Levi lowered his head and began to sob. Decades of pent up frustration bubbled to the surface.

"Levi …" Matt started, but found he did not have the words to go on.

"You have no idea what that man was really capable of. The things he did to me, growing up and as a man. Sure, maybe he stopped crawling into bed with me, but he ruined my adult life and my career." Levi's voice rose in time with his anger. His sobs gave way to rage.

"I'm so sorry. I could have helped, Mum and I, we could have helped," Matt began, but Levi looked at him with a flash of hatred, and it made his tongue fall still.

"Don't you dare be sorry. You have no right to be sorry for me. I'm glad that fucker is dead. To be honest, I was planning on killing him myself. I would have done so already if it wasn't for …wasn't for …" Levi stopped, catching his words. He stammered and spat a series of nonsensical sounds, clearly having said too much.

"What is it?" Matt pushed.

"Sorry to break up this little party, but we need to move. The locals seem to be gathering and I don't really want to get in their way," Finn spoke, the edge had fallen from his voice, softened in light of the harsh reality of their existence.

Matt got to his feet and looked around. The valley was enormous, showing the full scope and size of the world they were in. He could hear the rumble of a waterfall, the distinctive crash of cascading water on rock.

The ground shook at regular intervals, accompanied by a regular thudding noise. Looking back across the valley, beyond the large lake and over the grasses, he saw them. Enormous beasts, too large for his mind to even fathom or quantify. Their bodies were as large as houses, their necks as long as building cranes. Their legs were short and squat, just tall enough to keep the swollen belly of the creatures he assumed at first glance to be females, from dragging along the ground. Each giant step they took ushered forth a tremble in the earth and a rumble in the air.

"They are—"

"Argentinosaurus," Matt finished Ambrose's sentence for him. "I don't need a fancy watch for this one. They were the biggest creatures to ever walk the earth." There was a fascination to Matt's voice.

They moved in a herd, he counted at least twelve, including several that were much smaller than the rest. Juveniles, or so he assumed. They were quiet and methodical, a bulky grace to their movements that seemed to amplify their peaceful nature.

"They are magnificent," Matt spoke in a whisper.

A silence swept over the group, as they stood in awe of the world around them. There was no hunting, no death, merely the spectacle of the true great old ones, those that had been before.

"They are that," Ambrose agreed.

"Keep your eyes peeled, just because these boys are friendly doesn't mean there are not a dozen others waiting in the grass." Finn resumed his command.

"Where do we go from here?" Matt asked.

"The way I see it, we have two options," Finn began. "We can either carry on heading east, and move around the hunting trail we had designed, or we double back on ourselves, find a way up and backtrack towards the Spider." Finn pointed in a number of directions, as if he knew exactly where they were.

"What would you suggest?" Matt pushed.

"Well, we can't stay here, and we know what is waiting back that way. The blood we spilled will attract others. I say we push on through the valley, head up the cliffs at some point and come around behind those things and head home." There was a tone of uncertainty in Finn's voice. Matt picked up on it, but said nothing.

"Then we do that." He nodded and looked across at his brother in support.

Levi was struggling. That much was clear. He stood with his arms folded, stubble covering his face. He kept his eyes fixed on the floor and swayed from left foot to right foot and back again. He had pulled away from the group, and stood just to one side.

"You keep an eye on him now," Finn growled once more, looking Matt in the eyes while he pointed at Levi.

"I will do my best," he replied, nodding.

In the distance, the herd of argentinosaurus had spread out. They slowly wandered through the valley, stopping so that they could graze on the trees and vegetation the valley had to offer.

The group moved cautiously, not wanting to stick to the perimeter in case something was lurking in the thick trees that hid the steeply sloped banks, but at the same time, walking in the open felt as if they were exposing themselves too much. The grass was waist high in some places, and they all knew any number of creatures could be hiding there.

The day grew hotter as they moved. While the tall trees provided some shade, the layout of the valley and the presence of the same trees, seemed to pull the heat down and trap it. The air was heavy and stale tasting.

They had drawn level with the argentinosaurus herd. Matt had counted fifteen in all, including six juvenile beasts, ranging from the size of a giraffe to that of a double-decker bus.

The juveniles moved around among themselves, less interested in feeding than they were in what Matt assumed as a form of play. To him it looked as if they were playing a game of tag. One would reach forward and place its head on the base of another's neck. That seemingly passed the baton for that dinosaur to search out another in order to return the favour.

Behind the herd were other dinosaurs, smaller creatures with thin wiry bodies. They seemed to flock after and around the enormous sauropods. They ran in a flock of at least fifty, but with their speed and frantic movements it was impossible to get an accurate count.

Once they were up close to the large dino herd, the true size of the beasts could be appreciated. Their sheer bulk was stunning to behold, and their skin was not smooth as many pictures would have people believe, but rather it was covered in ridges, that appeared almost like stripes running over their flank. Hardened ridges of scaly skin provided extra protection from anything brave enough to prey on the creatures. Long deep gouges and healed wounds marred the bodies of the larger creatures, telling the tale of how rough life was, even for the largest creatures on the planet.

The group stopped walking, much to Matt's initial relief. His ankle felt as if it had been replaced by a ball of fire. Ahead of them, Finn crouched down in the grass, and instinctively, the others followed suit.

A few seconds later, the first dinosaur appeared. It ran from the trees and gave a high-pitched battle cry. It ran towards one of the smaller argentinosaurus which, even at the size of a truck, was much larger than the creature attacking it.

The dinosaur in question was not much taller than a man, but had a long tail that extended behind it for more than the length of its body. The creature was covered in red feathers, and seemed to glide on the air as it sprang towards its prey.

The young dinosaur cried out as eight-inch claws tore into its neck. The feathered dinosaur climbed like a parrot to the top of the long neck and bit down on the animal's head. Its jaws opened, and from such a close distance, Matt could make out a double row of teeth. The dinosaur shook its neck and tried to free itself from its attacker, but no sooner had it fought for its freedom, three others appeared from the grass. With the odds of four against one, the fight was a quick one, even if the death was slow. The dinosaur had a squeal to it that sounded like a cry. It was in pain and while the adults turned their attention to the problem, their sheer bulk made any movement a slow and methodical event. They were as useless to offer protection to their young as Matt and the group were to join in the fight.

The attack caused a domino effect of panic, which ran through the giant sauropods through to the smaller creatures, who abandoned their flock and ran about in all directions, including towards the crouching group.

"Get down!" Ambrose called, throwing himself flat into the grass. The first wave of tiny dinosaurs leaped over the group, but as their panic grew, their movements drew the attention of the feathered hunters.

Matt was too slow to move when one of the creatures jumped into his arms, landing stretched across them. It remained that way for a moment but was soon frantically scratching and scrabbling to get out of Matt's grip. He let it go the way a man would drop an angry cat, pulling his arms away, letting the creature fall to the floor.

It landed heavily at his feet, but before it could right itself, the feathered creature—a Utahraptor, according to the watch the guards wore—was on it. The small creature didn't stand a chance. It was bitten in half by the powerful jaws, nothing more than a mouthful. The raptor raised its head, the hind legs and tail still hanging from its mouth. It regarded Matt with cold eyes.

Matt braced himself as the raptor extended its large blood-stained claw. It moved to jumped but Matt acted without thinking. His finger squeezed the trigger on the shotgun he was holding. The blast threw him backwards, where he landed in the grass amidst a shower of blood, bone and sticky globs of brain tissue.

"What the hell," Finn shouted, storming towards Matt, who sat on the floor, his hands trembling. The shotgun was gone, dropped the moment he fired. In its place was the raptor's lower jaw which had been blown away by the blast.

Finn grabbed Matt and pulled him to his feet. "Run," he commanded, as the raptors began to descend on them.

Ambrose unleashed a burst from his M16, and while his well-clustered shot found their target, the raptor that fell had its place taken by two others.

"Move." Finn shoved Ambrose just as another raptor leaped towards them. He took it down with a shot to the leg, but his aim was off and all he did was wing the creature. More appeared from the trees, a large pack that had been lying in wait.

Matt ran as fast as he could. He was blind to the world around him. He was vaguely aware that there were people by his side, but in the moment they were shadows to him. Someone pushed him, directing him into the trees.

The ground sloped steeply upwards. Matt stumbled forward and fell to the floor. He landed on his hands and knees, pitched forward and hit his head against the hard ground. His vision went dark and then exploded with stars as the sounds of the jungle came back to him.

Matt turned around and saw Finn charging towards him, his face was streaked with blood. He ran and passed Matt without hesitation. Levi was not far behind, moving on autopilot, the same way Matt had been.

"Where's Ambrose?" Matt asked, but Finn was already gone, and Levi ignored him.

Matt moved a few paces down the slope, his field of vision clearing just enough to see the carnage he had caused.

Ambrose was standing just shy of the slope, his weapon raised. He turned in a series of sharp movements. First to the left and then to the right.

"Come on," Matt called. He could not see the threat that lay hidden in the grass. The three remaining Utahraptors leaped. Ambrose opened fire but missed. The large claw of the biggest raptor split Ambrose's head down the middle like a rotten grapefruit. The two halves of his skull teetered and then fell either side of his body, tearing his neck down to the shoulder. Blood fountained into the air like an ornate water feature in some fancy garden. Before Ambrose could even sink to his knees, the two remaining raptors each seized half a head and yanked it free of the body. The rest moved in just as Matt turned away.

He pulled himself away from the scene, but could not block out the sound of ripping flesh and crunching bone. Moving back up the slope, Matt found his pace slow. His legs were as heavy as iron and his vision clouded by tears. His hands shook so badly he could not even take a grip of anything to help support his climb.

Finn was nowhere to be seen, already at the top, no doubt. Levi was pulling himself up and over the edge, back onto the level ground. Matt was half way, at the point where the slope became its most severe. He struggled and grunted, inching his way to the top, surrounded by ferns and other plants. They served as a help as much they did a hindrance. The long, wide leaves of the ferns refused to move out of the way, and took a lot of energy to reposition in order to grant safe passage. The other dominating plant sort was of a much lighter weight but the underside of the leaves were coated with fine, hair-like thorns that burned when they touched the skin.

By the time Matt was reaching for the top, his whole arm was red and starting to swell. Exhaustion swept through him in paralysing waves. His arms ached from the poison the plants were seeping into his system, and his brain was talking to him, telling him it was his fault, and to just let go.

He did not dare chance a look behind him; he was terrified of what he would see.

His foot slipped and the vine he reached for came away from the wet ground. For a moment, Matt was suspended in the air, not falling, but incapable of preventing it nonetheless.

A hand shot out from over the edge of the cliff and took hold of his wrist. Pain exploded as a result of the burns, but he didn't care. Finding traction for his feet, Matt pushed with his legs and cried out as he was pulled over the edge.

He lay on the jungle floor panting. His teeth were gritted from the pain. He looked around expecting to find Finn standing at the ready, prepared to berate him once again. Only, it was a stranger's face that stared at him. One covered with blood and grime.

"Who …" Matt tried to asked, but words failed him.

The last thing Matt thought before unconsciousness claimed him was why the man who had saved him was holding his cock in his hands.

CHAPTER 9

"We've lost another three signals. Something bad is happening out there," Julian called out. Not that it was necessary. Tracy was watching the same screens he was.

"What is happening?" Tracy asked as she frantically turned dials and changed settings, testing to make sure the readings were genuine and not because of readout displays.

"They are in a dangerous world, Ms. Van der Meer," Albert Wilhelm III spoke up. He had spent most of the morning with them, but they had forgotten his presence. Tracy jumped when she heard his voice.

"You don't say," she snarled. "There must be something we can do. I mean, people are dying. Your guests, your people …" she began, but her words were being drowned out by a rage she struggled to control. She remembered Luc's warning to them, to not trust Albert, but also not to cross him.

"What she means is, maybe we could send in a rescue team, someone to go in and extract them. We could guide them to the exact location," Julian offered. It was a subject that he had been meaning to broach ever since Albert revealed his plans to them.

There was no contingency plan in place, no emergency procedures. If you got into trouble on the other side of the Spider, then you were on your own.

"There will be no rescue mission. The men all signed paperwork stating that they understood the risk of what they were undertaking." There was a calmness to Albert's demeanour. "There are always accidents and mishaps in the Beta trial phase. We will wait and see what happens, and make any adjustments I feel necessary ahead of the second round." He smiled at them. "Now please, return to your normal duties. I find it fascinating to watch how well you work together."

Julian and Tracy turned their back on the man, reticent to do so through the simple mistrust that they shared for him.

"We should tell him," Tracy whispered.

"Never, if it is what I think it is, then I'm not saying a damned thing to that son of a bitch." Julian answered, his voice stern , something that was uncharacteristic for him. Tracy understood, and nodded.

They worked in silence, checking and rechecking the same readings and settings. Finding things for them to do, so that they did not have to stop and risk engaging with their employer.

At some point during the afternoon, Albert left. A few hours later, he returned with a group of men, all wearing suits. There were six men that he addressed, and each of them had two bodyguards. Besides Albert, nobody spoke as they were shown around the lab. Albert made no attempt to introduce Julian or Tracy; in fact, he spoke as if they were not even there.

Julian could not fully make out the language that Albert spoke in, but it was a far cry from the well-spoken English that he was used to hearing.

After a while they left the lab, but a strange atmosphere remained. Both Julian and Tracy knew they would not sleep comfortably that night. The only solace they took was in the fact that Albert had revealed he knew of their love affair. It was all the confirmation they needed to move in with one another.

CHAPTER 10

Matt came to in the same place he had been when he passed out. The only differences being the stench of urine that hung over him like a cloud, and the fact that his every muscle in his body had decided to seize up together making any form of movement excruciating.

"We need to move," a heavy South African-lilted voice spoke. "Can you stand?" it asked.

Matt looked around and saw the same stranger who had pissed on him. His arm ... he remembered the pain and burning from the ferns. It was gone, his arm was still a little red but the worst of the pain and swelling were gone.

"Ambrose?" Matt asked, his brain still all at sea.

"He didn't make it. But we really need to move now, because that Finn guy did, and I don't think you are ready for that confrontation." The voice almost sounded entertained by the prospect. "Help me get him to his feet," the man asked, and suddenly arms appeared beneath each of Matt's and he was hauled into the air. His body sang out it agony, but much like a great and overdue stretch, the feeling that immediately followed up the pain was one of great relief.

"Who are you?" Matt asked, his head clearing by the second.

"My name is Luc. There is no time for that now, we need to move, get to some safety." The man felt Matt taking his own weight and slipped away from his support role. He had a rifle slung over his shoulder, and as he moved ahead of Matt and his brother, swung the rifle into his hands. It was nothing special, a straight-forward hunting weapon, but Matt had the feeling Luc knew how to handle both it and himself.

They were no longer walking on the path that had been carved out, but rather through the trees and dense foliage. The ground was still soggy underfoot but once they got away from the cliff edge it seemed to grow a little more solid, like walking on the wet sand close to the beach, but not on the shoreline itself.

The jungle seemed to come to life around them. As they moved, all manner of small creatures and insects jumped to life and scurried away. Most were the size of tennis balls or footballs, and there was the odd dog or cat-sized creature, but all seemed docile and more importantly, terrified of the humans that had disturbed them.

"Where are you taking us?" Levi asked after a while. He had moved a little behind Matt, his pace slowing compared to that of his brother, which was increasing.

"There is a patch of rocks not far ahead. They will give us some shelter to talk," Luc answered without turning around. "There is a lot to explain," he added, and Levi swallowed hard.

The patch of rocks was more a small mountain in Matt's eyes, but he was not going to argue semantics with the man that had saved his life. They scrambled up the face of the rocks, using footholds created by the formation itself. Rising about fifty feet or so, they came across a small cave-like opening in the face of a giant boulder. The rock itself was the size of a small house and while the space provided by the cave was not extensive, it gave them enough room to walk in—on a crouch—and sit without too much discomfort. Matt noticed a pile of burned sticks and ash at the mouth of the cave, along with the bones of several small creatures.

"How long have you been out here?" he asked, studying the pile of bones.

"Not as long as I would imagine. This place takes its toll fast, and if you don't adapt at an even quicker pace, then you will never survive." Luc sat down and leaned back against the rocks.

Matt did the same, although he feared he would not find it as comfortable as Luc appeared to.

"Who are you?" Matt asked. Levi had sat down beside him, his knees pulled up to his chest, his head then resting on his knees.

"My name is Luc. I was one of the three leads on the Spider project," he began.

"You're a scientist?" Levi spat, followed by a chuckle that was tinged with the graceful caress of madness.

"No, I was … I guess you could say that I worked as security for the two lead scientists. You see it was only the three of us there. We had been given our mission and an unlimited budget. The others, I'm sure you met them. Julian and Tracy were their names. They were my friends. Julian and I go way back. When the job came up, he called me to help." Luc smiled at the memory.

"You were employed to make dinosaur safaris?" Matt couldn't believe that was the truth, but the world was a crazy place, and the less logical the answer was, the more often it was right.

"No, we were employed as a team in an experiment. We had a theory to prove. If possible, the Spider would open up a whole new world of resources. You see, this does not travel through time, but through dimensions. This world is a mirror image of the one we call home, but it is just one of an infinite number of worlds from an infinite number of points in history that exist within each other. I'm not talking the stars and galaxies. That is many levels above this. Every single planet has this same construct, worlds within worlds. The options it would give us were vast." As Luc spoke, it became clear that he was far more than just the meathead his well-muscled frame would lead people to believe.

"So what happened?" Matt found himself drawn into the tale.

"Money happened. Money and greed. Some rich bastard bought us. Well, not us as individuals, but as in the project. He bought the concept of everything, including our servitude. They sent me here because I knew too much. I had worked with some of the mercenaries before, and their leader, well, I disliked him from the start. I learned part of the truth and they needed to get rid of me."

"What was the truth?"

"Why don't you ask your brother here?" Luc turned his head and stared at Levi.

"Me?" Levi snapped his head to attention.

"Yeah you. I've been watching you since you arrived, and man, you and your old man didn't keep much a damned secret," Luc growled, his anger clear.

"What do I know about this place?" Levi stammered, looking around him nervously.

"I am sure you met our rich benefactor, right?"

"You mean that Wilhelm guy?" Levi asked.

"Yes."

"He met us when we arrived. Why? I have no idea who he is."
Levi stared at Luc, whose eyes were locked on him. "I mean it.
I've never even heard his name before," Levi insisted.

"But what about the name Silvetti?" Luc asked, and Levi
jumped. His physical reaction to the name spoke volumes, and it
was something that even Matt noticed.

"How do you know that name?" Levi asked. His tone had
changed, his voice dropped in pitch.

Matt watched the two men, studied the way they were facing up
to one another. It was tight in the cave for all three of them, and all
of a sudden it became a much smaller space. If felt as if the walls
were closing in on them.

"How I know it is not of any importance. I know a lot of things.
A lot. What you need to tell me, is what you know about him."
Luc's face was a picture of intensity.

"He … It's nothing. It certainly doesn't have anything to do
with this place." Levi wormed his way around, looking for an
escape.

Matt's interest had been piqued. "I don't know, maybe it's
important. I'd sure like to hear more," he interrupted, glad that he
was sitting closest to the cave's exit. He had a feeling this was a
conversation he needed to see through, and knowing his family,
they would look to run from the discussion sooner than thrash it
out.

For a while, Levi was silent. He sat with his legs drawn up to
his body. He stared at the floor where he pushed around a small
bone with his foot.

"You don't know me, but know this. I've done a lot of things
for a lot less information than this conversation will yield. I'm here
to help you, so don't lie to me." Luc's voice was no nonsense and
his eyes burned daggers into Levi.

When Levi raised his head, tears streaked his blood-and-grime-
covered face. "It was never meant to go down that way."

"What are you talking about? What is he talking about?" Matt
asked Levi then Luc, as if the newcomer had all of the answers.

"Matt," Levi's voice changed. A calm fell over him as he turned
to face his brother. "Living with Dad was not easy. He was a
violent man, and arguing against him was not an option. He would

destroy anybody that stood in his way. Personally or professionally." Levi's eyes were locked on Matt.

"I know what he was like, Levi," Matt began, but his brother raised a hand to silence him.

"I didn't want to join the police. I never did, but Dad forced me into it. Once I was there … I found out a lot of things. Things I wish I didn't know." Levi was struggling to find the right words, stalling for time, maybe in the hope that he would be able to skirt around actually defining the point.

"Your old man was a dirty cop," Luc said, filling in the blanks. He was no nonsense. He needed answers and would get them without playing games.

"Yes, he was dirty. A lot of them were … are, but he was the worst of them." Tears filled Levi's eyes as he continued to look his brother in the eye. "Dad was involved in a lot of stuff, drugs and prostitution being the biggest things. He was an orchestrator, ensuring things slipped under police attention or went missing from the evidence room. There is a whole chain of command and he sat at the top."

"What about you, Levi? Were you dirty too?" Matt was also no longer in the mood for games.

"Come on, man," Levi tried to laugh, but his brother's stern gaze silenced him. "Yes." He lowered his head and sobbed. "Dad brought me into it pretty early on, and over the years … well, it's an addictive lifestyle. I know it was wrong, but I couldn't help it. The money, man, the money," Levi floundered.

"You son of a bitch," Matt spat getting to his feet, stooping because of the restrictive height of the cave.

"Matt …"

"Is that how he paid for this trip?" Matt asked, slapping away his brother's hand when Levi held it out to him.

"That's not important. The trip would have happened had your father had the money or not. Who was Silvetti?" Luc interrupted. "Was he going to rat you out?"

"Of sorts. He was a drug dealer. The main contact that my dad used for cocaine shipments." Now that he was cornered, Levi spoke with an easy, almost casual air to his words. He could no longer run and hide.

"What happened, he screw you over?"

"No, we screwed him. Dad got greedy, taking more and more over the years. One day, he decided to take things up a notch. He collected the shipment and then refused to pay full price. He was going to halve it, delivery fifty percent to the channels we had and then feed Silvetti to the lions, keeping the other half to sell himself. He would have tripled his money. I told him not to."

"Why did you suddenly develop a conscience?" Luc spat, stealing the very thought from Matt's mind.

"I was dirty, sure. But I played by the rules. Dad lost sight of that. Silvetti saw through the plan. He was on to us from the start. So Dad ... Dad shot him in the head and we dumped his body in the river. Dad took the drugs and claimed Silvetti never showed. That was almost eighteen months ago. We made a small fortune on that deal. It changed the game, and Dad just grew more powerful." Levi shook his head. With his confession over, the logical side of his brain took control. "How is any of this linked to being here, trapped in a world of dinosaurs?" He looked at Luc, who sat with a large hunting knife in his hands. He turned the blade over and over his hands, starting at the metal as if in a trance.

"Silvetti was just a cog in the wheel. Much like you and your father. The best I could gather was that Wilhelm is mafia. I'm talking high-level, deep-under-the-radar kind of mafia. He is a man with more power spread over the globe than anybody has ever dared imagine. From real life to fiction, nobody has as much influence or money as this guy. One nod of his head and the president could be dead, if he wanted it." Luc, who had stared at the knife while he spoke, looked up and his eyes were piercing daggers aimed at Levi. "Silvetti was not only one of his facilitators, but supposedly his cousin, and closest relative."

"How do you know all this?" Matt stepped in. "I mean ..."

"Don't worry. I'm on your side. I just got on the wrong end of the information and got trapped here the same as you." He turned his attention to Matt, and his voice changed. "I know you have nothing to do with this. They knew you were coming, but hoped to keep you separate, out of the way. They were going to kill you, but only to make a point." Luc turned his attention back to Levi, and anger filled his words once more. "I overheard some things and put the rest together myself. I got pulled away from my friends and sent here to die. Lucky for me, they were so focused on killing you, that they overlooked my history. I found a way to escape their death trap, and now I plan on getting out of here." He spat at the ground and stabbed his knife down with it.

"You mean to tell me that they did all of this, created a whole new world, not to mention a time machine, just to kill me and my dad?" Levi asked incredulous to the last.

"It's not a time machine. It is a portal. We are not back in the dinosaur age, we are in a different world, on a different level of existence, but I don't have time to discuss that right now. This is part of a much bigger plan, but killing you was high on Wilhelm's list. Even from the few conversations I overheard, his hatred for you was clear." Luc rose to his feet.

"So what, you're going to rescue us and turn me over to him again?" Levi refused to back down. He was in a corner and saw no way out.

"I'm getting myself and your brother out of here. You, you can die right now for all I care. Once I get back to my world, I'm going to do what I do best, but that is none of your concern."

"If he doesn't kill you, then I will," Matt growled, his voice taking both men a little by surprise.

They turned to face him, and saw he was holding a revolver aimed at his brother's chest. "All I have to do is pull the trigger." He tried to sound tough, but even he didn't truly believe it.

"Hey, put that down. We don't need the attention. That Finn guy is still out there, and he is a nasty piece of work." Luc moved towards Matt, his hands held out and open.

"Oh, Matt won't shoot. He doesn't have it in him." Levi laughed and watched as the gun began to tremble, shaking violently in his brother's grip.

Luc moved like the wind and took the gun from Matt. He then balled his fist and punched Levi in the gut. The man doubled over, coughing and wheezing as all the air his lungs could hold was forced from his body. His face turned red as he fell to the floor unable to breathe. "Next time you piss me off, it will be hot lead filling your gut, and that's a kind of pain that never quits," Luc growled, sliding the weapon into the waistband of his trousers. "Come on, we need to get moving."

The day was moving quickly, and the heat seemed to be even more cloying than the previous day. Moving through the trees was hard work. The vegetation was thick and the ground soft beneath their feet. Bugs and insects scurried along the floor, crossing their path every other step, or so it looked.

"Where are we going?" Levi asked.

"Back to the Spider. Now be quiet. You will give our position away," Luc snarled.

They walked in silence for the most part, Luc leading the way, Matt behind him, and Levi behind. Neither man paid him any attention, and had he fallen behind completely, or even turned and run, then neither would have cared either way.

Matt knew that they were being followed. He could hear the hurried footsteps of whatever it was rushing alongside them. He presumed Luc knew it also. It was hard to imagine him surviving alone for so long if he didn't. As long as their guide kept walking then Matt was content to keep moving. Every now and then he looked over his shoulder. His brother was keeping pace, but he felt nothing for him. He didn't want to keep him safe, but checked on him through habit. He was in their party and want him there or not, they needed to work together.

Beside them, the rustling stopped.

"Keep an eye open. There is something out there," Luc whispered, acknowledging their stalker for the first time.

They moved slower, and stopped between two large trees that were covered with long, slimy vines.

"Don't touch those. That sap is a paralytic of sorts. It won't kill us, but it will put your arm to sleep for a good twelve hours," Luc offered.

"How do you know?" Levi asked without thinking.

"Want me to show you?" Luc growled his response, irritated by the sound of Levi's voice.

Using the barrel of his M16, Luc pushed the vines apart, creating a gap for them to move through. No sooner had he done that, a small dinosaur sprang through. The creature was small, no more than a meter from the ground to the top of its head, but as skinny as a whippet. Its long, flat snout was filled with small teeth. It snapped at Luc, who swatted the creature to one side with the side of his hand.

More appeared, flooding through the vines. Luc pulled his M16 away, and the vines closed on the body of one of the creatures. Its pale white flesh was instantly marred by thick red prints.

The creature turned towards Matt and stumbled a few paces. It opened its mouth and lunged. The jaws closed around Matt's arms, which were reflexively raised to protect himself. The teeth were sharp, but like that of a puppy. They posed no threat to breaking the skin, and if anything, tickled.

The creature grew more and more sluggish as the paralytic took hold and eventually fell to the floor, its limbs still flailing. There was no time to rest, however, as no sooner had that one fallen, more appeared. They came from all angles, overpowering them with their numbers.

"Get off me." Matt swiped out and slapped one of the creatures away. He took a step back as they advanced on him. He slipped, tripping over his brother's feet.

The ground was soft squelched as he fell. It stank heavily of ammonia, and it conjured an image of two cats Matt had had when he was still living with his mother. They had taken to marking their territory in the house. Ultimately, they were rehomed, but Matt would never forget the smell.

"We should move out of their way," he called, as he swatted away two more creatures.

"What?" Luc called as he kicked out at a larger one of the dinosaurs, punting the side of its head with his military-grade boots.

"This is their territory. We need to fall back, or something," Matt tried again, backpedalling as a line of creatures advanced on him.

Beneath his feet, something snapped. It was a wet sound, but had a crispness to it, like a twig breaking underfoot. The creatures all froze, their jaws open as if in shock. They turned their attention to Matt, who looked down. There was an egg beneath his feet. The shell was crushed, and the gestating dinosaur foetus that had been growing within it also lay squashed beneath his sole.

"Run," he called, just as the small dinosaurs attacked. They made a strange whistling sound as they moved. Their rage undeniable.

"We're surrounded," Levi added. He had already turned to run before Matt had given the command, but had come face to face with a third group of the same dinosaurs.

Luc unsheathed his hunting knife and began to slash away at the creatures that, in spite of their numbers, were no genuine threat to the group. Heads rolled and fell to the floor in a shower of hot blood. The meaty scent filled the air, and Matt knew that he had no choice. He too had a knife, given to him by Ambrose before they climbed down from the trees. Pulling it from the waistband of his trousers, it shook in his grip.

A dinosaur lunged at him, and he stabbed out, impaling the creature through the throat. Instinctively, he pulled the knife away, and the creature expunged a shower of blood through the hole the blade had created. Death was not quick. The dinosaur ran around in all directions, thrashing and colliding with its brothers, coating them with blood, like war paint before it finally fell still.

Luc was moving. He slashed at the hanging vines and cut them down. He grabbed the limp body of one of the dinosaurs and leaped through, tearing the remaining vines free.

"Come on," he called.

Matt turned and followed, still holding the knife. Two dinosaurs moved towards him and he slashed wildly again, cutting them both, but neither wound did anything but stun the creatures and cause them to hold their distance.

Matt held the knife and jumped through the hole Luc had created. He heard Levi stumble behind him.

They emerged into a large opening, the trees long since felled. Rotted stumps sprouted from the ground, the dead wood wet and crumbling.

That was not the only thing.

"So this is what they were protecting." Matt looked around the clearing. Eggs littered the floor. Small white balls that looked like mushrooms lay all over the place. There was no nesting or apparent order to things. The eggs gave the impression of being laid wherever they were dropped.

"Shit, try not to break anything," Luc said as he looked around him. "We need to move across and into the cover of the trees." He was panting and breathing heavy from the skirmish, but much like Matt and Levi, he was unharmed.

The dinosaurs stood in a group, watching the three men. It was as if they had given up the fight. Their breeding ground had been breached. Resistance had no point. Matt could feel the weight of their gaze as he stepped over the eggs. He looked back as he neared the end of the field.

The first few dinosaurs had made strides towards their undisturbed eggs. Matt watched them, hoping that they understood, on some level at least, that he and the others meant no harm.

The trio disappeared into the trees and were once again swallowed up by the jungle.

CHAPTER 11

Julian lay in bed with Tracy beside him, the warmth of her naked flesh rubbed against his own. Placing an arm around her, Julian pulled her close to him, his own body tingling at the contact with her skin.

They had made love every night since they had moved into the same room, and as their passion grew, they became less shy about hiding their relationship, whether it be cuddling at the work station or the increased volume of their lovemaking, they no longer cared who saw, heard, or knew.

They needed something to keep them grounded in the real world. They had been underground for so long, they were starting to forget what it was like to be free. To take the subway to work, or to sit in the evening watching a movie and having a glass of wine. Wine other than the strange boxed stuff that Albert had permitted them to have delivered along with the weekly groceries.

They were forced to cook their own meals, as there were no other staff members on site, but both Julian and Tracy knew their way around a kitchen, so it was seldom an issue.

Julian listened to Tracy sleep. The gentle snores of her slumber. He kissed her naked back and cupped her ass cheeks with his hand. He was content in that moment. He did not need the sleep he had sought so long as he never needed to move from his position.

Sighing, he got out of bed, and quietly dressed so as not to wake Tracy. He slipped out of the door, and headed towards their kitchen area for a drink.

It was a little after two in the morning, and the facility should have been silent. Yet the sound of approaching footsteps was unmistakable.

Julian scrambled away and hid in the kitchen just in time.

The group of men entered, and the light was turned on just as Julian closed the door to the pantry he had slid into. The door was ajar, just slightly. Not enough to be noticeable.

Albert came in first, his wheelchair gliding silently over the floor. The other men in suits, the same ones he had shown around earlier that day, followed behind him. They moved through the kitchen, taking the glasses and cups they needed before settling down at the table to talk.

Julian held his breath. There was something about them that terrified him. He knew that if he was caught, as innocent as his presence was, it would not end well for him.

"So your problem has been taken care of?" one voice asked. It spoke with a heavy accent that Julian just couldn't place.

"As good as, yes," Albert answered. "I know it cost us some time, but it was of importance to me. They killed my cousin, my flesh and blood."

"We understand. The family bond is sacred," a second voice answered.

Julian was caught. He wanted to move away from the door, to sink further into the darkness, but there was a risk of making a noise that would draw attention to himself. Also, having heard the start of their conversation, he was intrigued as to where the rest of it would head.

"The good news is that my scouts have confirmed that the plantations are looking good. The local wildlife is easily kept at bay, and we have plans to introduce aerosol deterrents, not to mention the armed guard rotations," Albert spoke in a business-like tone. Gone were the snake-like expressions and the ulterior motives. He was in charge of this conversation.

"Mr. Wilhelm, with all due respect, I did not come here for a progress report. I have dealings back home that require my urgent—" The voice fell away to a gargle. A few moments later, a heavy thud came from the kitchen.

"I do hope none of you have a similar dissatisfaction with my calling this meeting," Albert spoke with a calm that gave Julian chills. The pantry where Julian hid grew warm. He started to sweat. It dripped from him, and ran into his eyes, but he dared not move to wipe his brow.

"No, sir. We are happy to be here. We are excited to understand more about the project and of course, the numbers that go with it," a third, more European voice answered. Julian thought French, but it could just as easily been Italian or even Dutch. It was mainland continent in any case.

"The numbers will still be set within the budgets we discussed last time. The location and the unique way in which I can deliver the product will see your initial costs go down, because product supply will be that much greater," Albert answered them.

Slowly, the conversation developed, and the business talk came into play. Julian drowned it out. He knew what he needed to know. He understood why Luc had been so concerned for their safety. All Julian wanted to do was to get out of the pantry, get to Tracy and take her to safety. He would do whatever was necessary.

Julian moved slightly, a cramp in his foot causing his left leg to jerk. He kicked at the door. It was a gentle connection that was drowned out by the sound of the conversation, but it made his heart freeze in his chest.

Time wore on. Julian had no idea how long it had been, for his watch lay on the cabinet beside the bed. The bed where Tracy still lay sleeping. At least, he hoped that she was sleeping still. He did not want her to wake and come looking for him.

Sinking to the floor, Julian closed his eyes and waited. He had heard enough to confirm his fears. Their new boss was not to be trusted, and so long as he and Tracy were in the facility, they were in grave danger.

After what felt like an eternity in the darkness of the pantry, Julian heard the chairs scrape along the floor. This was followed by the sound of footsteps echoing through the empty kitchen area. Conversation was over, there was no room for small talk among the men involved.

Julian did not want to move straight away. He knew he needed to give it time for the coast to clear, so he forced himself to be still. He focused on counting; the slow methodical plod through numbers had always helped him find his focus. Ever since childhood, he had drawn a calm from their constant, their certainty. Numbers were a fact, and facts could be relied upon.

Once he felt as if he had waited long enough, Julian stumbled out of the pantry. His legs were heavy and slow to respond to his commands. His eyes were growing heavy also, as the silence brought on the sleep that had eluded him for so long.

Julian staggered down the corridor and back to his room, finding his way in the dark without trouble. He didn't think about the others that had been there, or if they were still nearby. Everything he had heard had overloaded his brain and all he wanted to do was find Tracy, curl up beside her and sleep. He would make a more affirmative decision once the sun rose.

Tracy had not moved; the blanket was still pulled back, revealing the flesh of her back and the curve of her buttocks. Julian closed and locked the door to his quarters, let out a long sigh and slid beneath the sheets, curling up with the woman he loved.

Sleep came, but it was not a completely restful one. He had heard too much to ever sleep soundly in that place again.

CHAPTER 12

"We need to find some weapons," Luc said as they all crouched down behind the large leaves of a giant fern.

"I don't think we stand a chance fighting against the dinosaurs," Levi answered, a little too loud.

As they had walked, Matt had noticed his brother change. He became less concerned with concealing his movements, and keeping noise to a minimum. It was as if he were ignoring the fact that they were walking through a humid hell that wanted to kill them every step of the way.

"It's not them I'm worried about. It's him," Luc whispered, pointing ahead through the fern, beyond the steaming pile of dung that had led to their seeking a hiding place.

Beyond the shit heap, which had been left by an enormous, spiny-backed dinosaur with a large knotted club-like tail, they saw a figure running through the trees. The man was limping and carried his arm clutched tight against his body. He was shirtless, said shirt having been used to restrain the injured arm and prevent it moving even further.

Matt caught his breath. They waited, and a moment later, a series of grunts rang out. They were not the cacophonous grunts of a hungry therapod, but rather a group of strange, boar-like creatures. They emerged from the jungle, the bodies coated in black fur. Their snouts were buried in the ground and they ran as a group towards the steaming tower of excrement. Their grunts turned to excited squeals as they buried themselves in it, devouring the larger, undigested lumps of whatever it was that the spiny dinosaur had evacuated from its bowels.

"Let's move around. Keep quiet and stay in a single line. That man is hurt, but that just makes him more dangerous," Luc instructed, not looking back. He never took his eyes away from the jungle.

Moving around the feasting boar family brought the group back within sight of the trail that had been cut for them.

"There is a weapon's cache near every hunting station," Matt offered, speaking up as they stopped once again.

Luc was keen to never move more than a few hundred meters without stopping and reassessing the lay of the land.

"I know," Luc responded curtly. "There is one just up ahead, but I am afraid our friend has already beaten us to it. He was injured. He will be locked away trying to patch himself up," Luc spoke, his eyes constantly moving over the jungle.

The longer they spent there, the more Matt became adjusted to it, and the more he could hear the never-ending sounds of life. It was all around them. Rustling from creatures high up in the trees, which towered over their heads like skyscrapers in a big city's business district. There was a buzz in the air from the insects and creatures that flew on heavy, beating wings, or in the crackle and snap of felled branches and trees as larger dinosaurs made their way along whatever path it was they had decided to follow.

Matt looked over his shoulder and saw that Levi had stood up behind them. His eyes were fixed on the hunting area and cabin that lay beyond. He had a glassed over look in his eyes. It was the look of a man who saw no other way out.

It reminded Matt of the faces he saw coming through the hospital doors some days. It was the look of the dying. Those who knew that death was coming for them, whether through a terminal illness or because of some other kind of sickness, one that had them believing there was no other way. He could always tell the difference between those that spoke of death, and those that truly welcomed it. Everything could be seen in a person's eyes.

"Levi ..." he began, knowing that it would do no good, but also understanding how important it was that he try; for himself as much as for his brother.

"I'm sorry, Matt ... I've failed in everything. I couldn't protect you. I lost you as a brother, and I lost you as a friend. I have nothing to go back to." Levi turned his head and looked at his brother. Even if his eyes did not truly focus on him, the intent was clear.

"There's another way, brother," Matt offered, but Levi paid it no mind.

Levi strode towards his baby brother and threw his arms around his neck, hugging him tight, and hard.

"I love you, Matt. I always did," he whispered, kissing the side of his brother's head before he took off through the trees.

"Levi …" Matt whispered a little louder than he should have.

"Let him go, man," Luc answered. "There was nothing you could say to hold him back." For the first time since they left the cave, Luc turned and looked at Matt. "I'm sorry," he added, with genuine emotion.

"What do we do now?" Matt crouched back down behind the felled tree trunk that had sheltered them.

"We wait, and you can hope that your brother comes out of this in one piece," Luc answered, his eyes once again focused on the jungle.

Levi was absorbed by the trees and when he re-entered their field of vision, he had his revolver drawn. He moved at a pace between a run and a brisk walk, a heavy limp to his gait. He moved his way up the steps to the hut, pulled open the door and disappeared inside. The sound of gunshots rang out, a series of pounding detonations within the cabin.

Matt tensed, and found he closed his eyes for some reason. It was only once the relative silence had been restored that he opened them. Luc had already made his move, so Matt followed.

They emerged from behind the tree and moved forward, keeping low on their haunches, towards the cabin. The commotion would have surely warranted some unwanted attention from the local wildlife.

The pair reached the cabin and climbed the steps. The smell of blood was heavy on the air, and made Matt's aching stomach retch. Maybe it was because the scent was family, his body reacted differently, he didn't know.

Finn lay on the floor, his body had been peppered with lead. It was impossible to count the exact number of shots, because his once muscular physique had been minced by the close grouping of bullets. He sat back against the wall, slumped to one side. The wall behind him showed the damage of the less accurate shots. His chest rose and fell in a jagged rhythm. Neither Matt nor Luc paid him much mind.

Seeing them, Finn tried for his gun, but the exertion was too much for him and with a final cough that showered blood from his blue-tinged lips, he died.

Luc was busy gathering weapons. Including a gun that looked similar to the construction of the electronic weapon Matt had first taken. Only this one was a lot larger. Luc's muscles bulged from the strain of picking it up.

Matt was not focused on weapons. He had turned his attention to his brother. Levi lay on the floor of the hut, his stomach ripped open by the burst of fire he had taken. His hands were clamped against the wound, but his insides still slid through his blood-soaked fingers, like fat sausages escaping their bag.

"I'm dying," Levi stated. His body trembled with shock.

"Yeah," Matt answered as he crouched down beside his brother. Reaching out, he took one of Levi's hands in his own. It was as cold as ice. "It's going to be okay. I'm right here, brother." Matt made no attempt to hide the tears that burned in his eyes.

"I don't want to die … I … I'm not ready to go to Hell," Levi sobbed, his breaths coming shorter and shorter.

"I'll leave you two alone," Luc said as he moved to the door of the hut.

"You're not going to Hell, man. Everything that happened. That wasn't your fault. You had nothing to do with it." Matt realized as he spoke that he truly meant what he said. As a doctor, there were many times when what the patient needed to hear was merely a comfort, a way of soothing them in their final moments. This time was not like that. This was one of the times that the words were genuine. Matt didn't blame his brother. He knew that he was a good person.

Levi opened his mouth, and his lips curled into a smile, but his final breath danced over his blood-smeared lips before he could say anything. His eyes stared hauntingly at his brother, who had lain him down and closed the lids.

"Sleep softly, brother," Matt whispered through his grief. He leaned over, kissed Levi on the forehead like a mother bidding her child good night, and then walked away.

Luc was waiting for him on the path, and said nothing as Matt wept while they walked.

CHAPTER 13

The jungle got no easier on them as they moved. The terrain grew worse as they reached the end of the trail.

"I thought this led back to the Spider?" Matt said as they stood on the end of the path. Ahead of them the jungle was thick and impenetrable, or so it seemed behind the wall of ferns that seemed to guard against further passage.

"It should, but they had also planned on you all being dead long before reaching this point," Luc answered coldly. "Come on, there is a river this way. We can wash up and follow that for a little. That will take us around the turn and leave us with another clearing to cross at the base of the volcano, where the Spider is," Luc instructed. He recited the terrain as if it were just like any other place he had ever given directions for.

The river began as nothing more than a small creek. Matt had seen larger bodies of water running through the streets after a heavy rain storm. Yet Luc stopped and took the time to splash his face and hold his head against the ground so that the stream ran over him.

"You are better to do it here. Trust me." He smiled.

Matt didn't question him. Not aloud at least. He bent down and copied Luc's movements with the water. It was cold, surprisingly so given the suffocating environment.

The change in the stream was so gradual that Matt did not notice it until it had become a raging torrent of water. The fast moving current could be heard as it barrelled its way to the waterfall, which Matt could hear but not see. The stream, which had become a river, turned around to the left and the end point was hidden by the dense vegetation.

"Looks like we are going to have to climb," Luc called back to Matt, as he had started to lag behind. The bumps and knocks he had taken, not to mention the strain or watching his family die, no matter how satisfying one of those deaths was, had begun to take its toll.

"What?" Matt wanted to fall to his knees as he saw the steep descent that lay in wait for him.

"Well, we could walk around, but I have no idea how far it is, or how long it will take, but I am going to guess that we wouldn't make it." Matt was not sure if Luc was being serious, or had just chosen a really bad time to inject humour into his conversations.

"I guess I don't have a choice," he said, resigned.

Luc went first, moving down slowly. The rocks were damp and in some places slick with an orange-coloured algae.

Matt lowered himself over a short while later, unsure if he even had the strength to make it over the edge of the drop.

"Be careful, some of these bastards are slippery as wet fuck," Luc called up to him.

"I'd noticed," Matt answered through a clenched jaw. A misplaced foot had already caused his heart to enter his throat.

The lower they climbed, the louder the roar of the waterfall became, but the two continued to descend, moving slowly and smoothly. There was a strange rhythm that appeared in their movements, and their descent became a sort of glide. Luc had the large weapon slung over his shoulder in a makeshift sling crafted from a vine, and showed no direct ill-effects from the extra weight pulling him to the ground.

"Get off me," Matt heard Luc call. "Ah, you motherfucker," he added shortly thereafter, only moments before he gave a cry as he fell from the rocks.

Matt looked down at the commotion and saw the scorpion jump from the rock and onto Luc's face. Its stinger swiping wildly, but the curve of Luc's head seemed to bring his skin out of range. As he fell, Luc swatted the creature away. He looked up at Matt, his eyes wide with fear. It seemed for a second as if he would never fall. Matt thought if he could move fast enough, he would reach Luc in time; that he could pluck him from the air.

The laws of physics won out, however, and Luc plummeted the final portion of their descent, crashing into the pool at the base of the waterfall.

"Luc ..." Matt called out, suddenly finding that his body could descend the rocks much quicker than it had before.

He moved fast, looking over his shoulder the whole time, studying the water for a sign of Luc's body.

With ten feet to go, Matt lost his grip, his hand sliding off an algae-covered rock. He fell through the thick ferns and landed hard on the soft ground. The wind was knocked from his body and his head crashed into the ground hard enough for him to see nothing but blackness with a smattering of shiny white stars. Shaking himself out of the daze, Matt scrambled to his feet. His head ached and his vision moved in and out of focus with a drunk's ease, but he was conscious of his surroundings.

He reached the river bank and began to call for Luc, who had still not surfaced from the water.

Wading into the pool, which had the surprisingly refreshing result of clearing his head somewhat, Matt continued his calling.

Luc broke the surface a few moments later, swimming for all he was worth. He frantically pulled himself to the bank.

"Get out of the water!" he yelled at Matt when he saw him. "Get out now!"

Matt responded immediately, watching Luc as he emerged from the water and ran for the trees. The large beast that followed him was a clear motivation for his retreat. The creature looked like a crocodile, but its jaws alone were the size of a normal croc's body. The large saucer-sized eyes dragged the long body out of the river and over the bank. Its nose reached the trees before its tail end fully emerged from the pool.

Matt, who had fled into the trees himself, guessed that the creature was around thirty feet long.

It sniffed at the air, slamming its long snout against the trees, but after a while it grew tired, and turned its frame around and slid back into the water. Matt could see the creature slide beneath the surface, and like a ghost it floated away. It didn't leave, however; rather, it sat, submerged, lying in wait. It knew that they would be back.

When Luc emerged from the trees, Matt wondered what he was doing. There was no way he had not seen that the creature was still there. Then he saw the gun, lying in the mud.

Luc edged slowly closer and closer, crouching as low to the ground as he could, walking with long strides that looked as awkward as they no doubt were. The weapon was midway between the trees and the water. A swift grab and a sprint would bring Luc back to the trees, but even Matt understood that the dino-croc would have no difficulty crushing a few trees with its bulk before it gave up the chase.

Luc reached the gun. His hands grabbed it and pulled it from the mud with a wet sucking sound.

He held it and watched the water. He knew. Matt knew. The creature burst from the pool, thrusting its body forward effectively leaping onto the land. Luc braced himself, armed the weapon, and pulled the trigger. For a moment, nothing happened. Then a bolt of blue fire, the electrical charge that Finn had mentioned to Matt at the start, burst from the rifle's barrel. It separated the creature's upper jaw, slicing through flesh and bone with ease, before detonating. Half of the creature was blown away in the blink of an eye. Large lumps of croc meat were sent flying in all directions, as the crack of the explosion whipped like a lightning strike.

The stench of roasted flesh filled the air, with the fetid aroma of rotting fish as a follow up flavour. Luc was thrown back by the explosion, and fell to the floor. The dino-croc was dead; there could be no question about it, as its head and half of its body were no longer there. The blast had torn the creature apart, and the portion that remained lay smouldering on the muddy bank.

Chunks of flesh rained down, dripping from the nearby trees like fat drops after a storm.

"Are you okay?" Matt walked towards Luc, stepping over or around the chunks of dead croc that littered his path.

"My hand," Luc grunted. "My hand is on fire. That damned scorpion sting." Luc closed his eyes as he fought against the pain.

Matt looked at the hand. It was black and festering. The ring from where the scorpion's tail had struck was clear. The inner part of the puncture wound had flowered outwards, pulling the raw meat of the hand with it. Thick yellow pus oozed from the center of the wound, like an erupting volcano. The flesh was rotting fast. The whole hand was gone, and it had started to spread to the wrist.

"I need to amputate," Matt answered. He knew there was no saving the hand, but the speed of the rot also left him with no time for tenderness.

"Do it," Luc grunted, his body contorting from the pain. "Just get it over with."

There was no anaesthetic at hand, and no way of sterilizing the large machete blade Matt would have to work with, but a secondary infection could be treated once they got back home.

"Hold still," Matt said as he gripped the blade. The edge was sharp, but not sharp enough. A swift powerful blow was what it would take.

Matt swung the blade and it sliced through the flesh with ease. The rotting tissue parted like warm butter, and the bone itself had been softened by the poison which made it easy to cut.

The hand fell to the ground and Luc cried out into the crook of the elbow on his other arm.

The weapon lay on the floor and Matt could feel the heat from the barrel from where the charge had been fired. It was not ideal, but it was all he had to stop the bleeding.

Using all of his strength, Matt pulled the weapon to him, hefted it into the air, and pressed the hot barrel against the wound. The sizzle of flesh was a good sound, because it meant that the effort was worth it.

The stump was cauterized and Matt used his own shirt to wrap the wound. He knew that infection was a guarantee, but had he not acted, Luc would have been dead long before they made it back to the Spider. When it came to action, Matt never second guessed himself. He trusted his training and his ability to judge the severity of the situation.

"Can you walk?" Matt asked after they had sat a while. Luc had passed out for a moment, but was sitting on the floor prodding his blackened hand with his foot. The rot had continued, and the severed appendage was already half liquefied.

"Yes, just help me up, would you?" Luc smiled as Matt helped haul him to his feet. "All the dinosaurs around and I lose my hand to a fucking scorpion. Do me a favour, when we get back, we are telling them it was a dino bite," Luc joked, and for the first time in a long time, Matt laughed. It felt great.

"Only one step to go, right?" Matt asked hopeful.

"Pretty much. There is a clearing up ahead, we need to cross that. It will bring us to the base of the volcano. Then it's just a scramble across to get to the Spider."

"How do you know it will work?" Matt asked, wondering for the first time how they would get home. "If we were supposed to die, what makes you think that it will be able to bring us back?

"Because I helped build the thing. Kind of. Two of my closest friends are running it. They have nothing to do with any of this. They were just scientists who got screwed over. They are there. They will see my vital signs on the monitors, and know what to do."

Matt didn't push it any further. He didn't have the energy.

They moved through the trees. Their pace slow. The heat of the jungle bore down on them, and in their condition, it became even more oppressive.

The sound of heavy thudding burst through the trees ahead of them. It was a dull, meaty thwack of a sound, and it was repeated every few minutes. The closer they came the louder the sound was, and with it came the now eerily familiar rumble of the ground.

"We should go around," Matt offered, before he had even seen what lay ahead.

"There's no time," Luc said, grimacing. He was sweating and looked like hell. Matt could tell that he was struggling more than he would let on.

Just ahead of them a tree cracked, the bough split and tore apart as the tree fell. It landed to their left. Not close enough to be a danger, but there was enough of that ahead. The felled tree created a gap in the jungle. They could see what was the cause of the damage. Two triceratops were rutting. They charged at each other, their heads colliding with the hollow clunk of horn followed up by the meatier impact of their skulls against one another.

Both were bloodied by the encounter, but neither seemed eager to quit.

"There must be female in the area. Watch out. Last thing we need to piss them both off and have them charging us down," Luc whispered.

As if on cue, the female triceratops moved through the trees beside them. She paid the men no mind. Her attention was focused on the strapping males that were vying for her affection.

"The female is over there, so if we wait for her to make an appearance, then run to the right, we can cut across their rutting ground and through into the clearing," Luc said, pointing and keeping his voice low.

Together, they watched and waited. The males made another line up against one another and charged. From their close proximity, the collision created a rumble that both men felt; it was a moving wall of air that delivered a punch to the surroundings. One of the triceratops gave a cry. The emergence of the female had shifted the balance slightly. One male shifted his head just a little, and one of the long upper horns punctured its neck. The wound was not fatal. It defined the winner of the fight, but both animals would live to fight another day.

"Now," Luc spoke, and they burst from the trees. Their emergence did not go unnoticed as had been their hope. The female gave a roar, one more deafening than her male counterparts, and the ground thundered as she gave chase.

"Run!" Matt cried. He didn't need to look over his shoulder to know what he would see bearing down on them. His mind conjured an image, and that was horrific enough for his tastes.

The two men sprinted across the small patch of jungle and disappeared into the trees. Behind them the crash and splintering of trunks told them that the girl would not give up without a fight.

"Split up, she can't follow us both," Luc wheezed. Matt looked at him. The man was struggling. His arm was bleeding again. He was pale and drenched in sweat. He had a sickly pallor to his skin.

They peeled away in different directions as the female caught up with them, charging headlong into the trees as they ran either side. With her prey gone, the triceratop's demeanour changed. She calmed and eventually stopped.

Matt saw that the beast had given up the chase, but he did not stop himself from running. He could no longer see Luc, and found his pace increased as a result. He wanted to put enough distance between himself and the dinosaur, so that he could safely double back and find Luc before it was too late.

The jungle thickened around him, and when Matt stopped running, he immediately lost all sense of direction. He turned and knew the way he had come, but the foliage was so thick around him that moving through it was like trying to find your way to a certain point in a pitch black room.

Matt forged his way on. His legs were heavy and it seemed as if every leaf and branch he needed to move weighed as much as a house and spawned double the number of leaves behind it.

The clearing appeared from nowhere, the thick foliage giving way to an area of lush grassland that extended as far as Matt could see.

The gathering of dinosaurs made the clearing with the argentinosaurus look like nothing. In every direction he turned his head, Matt saw herds of dinosaurs walking together. They stayed in their family units but he saw stegosaurus and other triceratops. He saw great sweeping bodies of smaller dinosaurs all intermingled as they sped around the plain darting through and around the legs of the giant diplodocus herds that were gathered around one the copses, eating their fill from the lush green leaves a the top of the tall trees.

It was an idyllic scene, and one that brought with it a strange sense of peace and tranquillity. There was a grace to the giant creatures, which could be felt as well as observed.

Luc crashed through the jungle, his bloodied and beaten body appearing through the foliage like a zombie through the trees.

"Come with me. I need to show you something," he gasped. He was out of breath, but there was a light in his eyes that had not been there before.

"What is it?" Matt asked.

"Answers," Luc said with a smile. He turned and disappeared through the trees. The jungle swallowed him whole, and Matt wondered how he was supposed to follow him.

The path was easy and short, however, because the dense jungle had been cleared away. The trees and been ripped from the ground, their roots removed and their tips cut into rough spikes. They had then been reinserted into the soft ground at an angle that would impale most things that came into contact with them. The space cleared was about the size of a football field. The ground had been turned and turned, cultivated. An area, Matt guessed around a quarter of the cleared space, had plants growing in it.

"What are they?" Matt asked, looking at Luc, who was walking up and down the plants, his hands running over the leaves.

"They are cocaine plants," Luc said, looking over at Matt.

"Cocaine?" Matt repeated.

"Yeah, they are pretty young, but there's no question about it. I think I know why they were so keen on the Spider. They–"

"They are going to grow their own drugs in here. That way they can control everything," Matt interrupted, showing that while his body was wrecked his mind was still sharp as a tack.

"Exactly. They will control quantity, quality, and price. It will bring a complete paradigm shift through to the drug world." Luc looked around, suddenly certain that they could not be alone.

"So this was all about money … revenge and money." Matt was gobsmacked.

"Well, isn't that how the world always works?" Luc moved away from the plants and back beside Matt.

"True. I think I'm more than ready to get out of here now."

Matt, too, felt the atmosphere change. The dinosaurs were one thing. They had survived that, so far at least. But knowledge was the biggest danger, and it was something that now transcended worlds.

"Me too," Luc answered.

The two men turned and walked back through the trees. Before they emerged back in to the clearing, Matt found himself checking his pistol. Luc had the dinosaur-exploding, electric rifle slung over his shoulders.

They worked together to push the remaining ferns aside and found themselves back in the clearing. The world had changed. The sky had darkened and the gathered clouds were swollen with an impending downpour.

The dinosaurs were still there, but they seemed to move with a greater urgency. The smaller creatures were gone, the diplodocus were moving away from the trees, their gait unhindered by the presence of the smaller creatures.

The lightning struck before the rain began to fall. A thick, blue streak that struck the central tree formation, splitting the bark of the unlucky tree all the way down to the root. Three more shafts of lightning were hurled towards the earth before the rain came.

"What do we do now?" Matt shouted to be heard above the deluge.

"We move," Luc answered as if it the question itself was an insult. "The volcano is just behind those trees. We can make it before nightfall." Luc was confident. Matt heard it in his words and felt it coursing through himself.

They kept to the trees, not venturing too far away from the jungle line. The rain fell in sheets and in no time the ground was a swamp. It sucked at their feet and tried to pull them down, but the men were not to be halted.

They reached a break in the jungle where the swamp gave way to the rocks of the volcano. Before they could set foot on solid ground, however, there was one final surprise for them. Thunder rumbled through the air, the deep growl travelling low over the ground. A van-sized therapod burst from the trees. It stumbled over the boggy ground, but did not fall. Out of the jungle, the creature appeared even more frantic and continued its charge across the open ground towards the trees on the other side. It ignored the other beasts it passed, paying them no mind in its panic.

The rocks were slick with rain, a fact only made worse given the stark contrast to the sticky grassland.

"We don't need to climb too far. The Spider unit was placed close to the jungle to give people a quick coverage. Of course, that was before they knew what else was out here."

"You hope," Matt added, feeling comfortable to express himself a little more.

Luc gave no answer.

The volcano rose above them, and while he knew better, Matt couldn't help but imagine that each rumble that ran through the ground was a result of the volcano growing irritated with their intrusion rather than through the storm.

The path they followed worked its way around the base of the fire mountain; their course staying as close to flat as was possible. The storm drowned out the sounds of the jungle, and the rain created surging streams that ran down the side of the volcano, crashing against them with enough force in some places to make them second guess their footing.

Had the wind not been howling, or the thunder not chosen that moment to rumble through the world, then maybe they would have stood more of a chance. As it was, they never saw the large, black-haired beast coming. Not until it was already upon them, and by then, it was too late.

CHAPTER 14

"We need to get out of here." Julian greeted Tracy as she woke.

Julian had not slept for more than an hour. He had spent the rest of the night packing his and Tracy's things. He did not plan on spending another day in the underground facility. He would rather wander the streets of Bloemfontein than he would carry on contributing to the destruction of the world.

"Good morning to you too," Tracy responded, confused. "You could at least offer me a cup of coffee before you hit me with holiday plans." She tried to make light of the situation.

"I'm not joking, Tracy. We are getting out of here today. I heard them last night. I know everything that is going on," Julian spat the words in a torrent.

Tracy got out of bed, pulling on a sweatshirt from the pile of clothes that were stacked in the corner ready to be thrown into a bag.

"Slow down, slow down." Tracy moved across the room and gave Julian a hug. "Start from the beginning."

Julian closed his eyes and took a deep breath. "I couldn't sleep, so I went to get a drink. While I was there, Albert came in, with those guys from yesterday. I hid in the pantry, and they were talking all about their plans. This place …it's all a front. This is just about drugs. They are going to grow drugs in the worlds the Spider links to Albert; he is some sort of mob boss," Julian exhaled. It sounded so stupid when he actually put words to his panic, but he knew what he had heard.

"You heard them?" Tracy asked thoughtfully.

"Yes, they were all sitting in a group. They chose those three men just to kill them. It was something personal, but deep down this is about drugs and money." Julian stared with wild eyes.

"What is your plan?" Tracy asked, not sparing a second to question Julian.

"I want to disable the Spider. Shut it down and fry the motherboards. We fuck it up, and leave when nobody is looking. I don't want to be part of this, but don't want my machine, my baby, being used by anybody if it means drugs." Julian found his resolve, and stood up straighter as he spoke.

"That's the man I love. Then let's do it. We head there, take it down and get out." Tracy leaned in and kissed Julian. She felt and tasted his fear. It comforted her to know he was so scared, because it meant he was acting on his convictions, not because he was getting cold feet on some project with which he had long been associated. "Luc told us that it was all about money. Do you think he found out?"

"I do now," Julian answered. He had forced himself to not think about his fallen friend too much.

They dressed and hastily packed the rest of their belongings, only taking the bare essentials. They needed a quick escape, and heavy bags would only slow them down.

It was still early, and when they entered the lab, it seemed even more empty and spacious than before. Their footsteps echoed louder, the every move was amplified.

They moved into position behind the console, and fired up the Spider. Dials flashed as the console whirred to life.

Julian and Tracy worked in silence, their dance was seamless and needed no commentary.

Tracy left the main controls to Julian, who would be the one to bring the levels to their maximum. He knew the subtleties of the Spider better than anyone, and could trigger her shut down with the least attention drawn.

"Julian, take a look at this," Tracy called to him, her voice shattering the silence.

"Is that ... no, it couldn't be." He caught his breath. "We have to power it up." He looked at her. "We can't leave them there." He stood firm.

"I know. But we can't wait for them forever." She looked at him. She knew that their actions would be traced, and their flight would be foreseen. Timing was their only advantage.

"Give me ten minutes. If they don't come through, we overheat it that way. We can explain ourselves by saying we had a reading at the extraction point. We still think this is a hunting trip." Julian worked the numbers in his head and began to reset the dials as he spoke.

A slow round of applause began. Each clap echoed around the lap. A figure approached them. Albert Wilhelm III emerged from the shadows, as was his way. His wheelchair was gone. He walked towards them. Striding on powerful legs.

"Well done, Dr. Grau, well done indeed." He smiled that reptilian smile which was cold and slimy to look at. "It is amazing the things you can hear when you pay attention to the signs. That pantry door was not as closed as you thought." The lips pulled back to reveal teeth too white to be real.

"What do you want?" Julian asked, determined not to be stopped.

"I want you to understand something. The two of you were safe. You had a job to do, and I had no intention of keeping your services any longer than necessary. You would have been free to go." Albert began to pace back and forth.

"Why don't I believe you?" Julian snarled.

"Well, the simple answer is that you no longer have to. You see, you betrayed me. You stand here whispering behind my back about shutting the machine down, about stopping everything I have worked so hard for. I cannot allow that. Such acts cannot go unpunished." Albert pulled a gun from the waistband of his trousers. In a single, emotionless movement, he raised his arm, stared Julian in the face and pulled the trigger.

The gunshot rang out, deafening in the lab. Julian flinched, while beside him, Tracy fell to the floor. Blood bubbled from her lips. Her body shook and trembled. Pink foam gathered in her mouth and spat from it as she coughed her final words. The bullet hole was neatly placed in the center of Tracy's forehead. A small, dark red, almost black wound. Blood leaked from the rear of her skull where the bullet had left a mark that was nowhere near as neat as its entry point.

"No … No, no Tracy …no." Julian fell to the floor, his knees splashing in the spilled blood. Julian grabbed her hand, but she was already gone. Her eyes stared blindly, her features in an expression of shock.

Julian lowered his head to her chest and felt his emotions swell up and collide. They came to a head and spewed from his lips as rage.

He turned and stared at Albert, who stood before the activated Spider. "You son of a bitch," Julian growled, making a move to charge the man down.

A second gun shot rang out, and pain exploded through Julian's body. The bullet missed its mark, but tore through his flank, sending him crashing to the floor. Pain lit up his world and removed all finer details. All he saw was Albert, smiling down at him, as he carefully took aim. Behind him, the red glow of the spider, his life's work, continued to grow. The orb, like a giant eye, watching its master burn.

Julian closed his eyes to block out the pain, and he heard Tracy's voice singing to him. Calling him. He lay down, and when the third gunshot of the morning came, he didn't feel a thing.

Chapter 15

The large, cat-like beast sprang down onto them. The only sound it made was an angry hiss upon landing. He was between the two men and needed to pick a side. Matt had fallen to the floor, fumbling for his gun, he found his hands, usually so steady in a stressful situation, refused to cooperate.

The beast, which was easily twice the size of a lion, had a long tail that whipped in the air. Long bristle-like hairs collected in a ball at the tip. Its fur was black, slicked by the rain so that even in the darkness of the storm, it seemed to shimmer.

The creature turned towards Luc, who had remained standing. He held the electronic pulse rifle in one hand and awkwardly tried to take aim. The mountain cat watched him, and gave an angry howl, swiping out with paws the size of dustbin lids. Nails at least six inches long, four to a paw, sprang from within its flesh and sliced at the air. Luc was out of range, but the beast was not to be deterred. It took a pace forward, hunting its prey.

"Brace yourself," Luc called as he pulled the trigger. The gun began to glow and fired a round. The weight of the gun was intense, and Luc's remaining arm, which was always his weaker arm, was unable to take the strain. His aim faltered just before the shot was emitted. The blue pulse of energy caught the beast in the flank, tearing away a thick strip of flesh and the red meat beneath, but given the heat of the blast, the wound was cauterized, or close to it.

The beast gave a roar and leaped forward. The claws from its front legs dug deep into Luc's torso, just beneath this shoulders. The rifle fell to the rocky ground and slid away. Luc collapsed under the weight of the animal, which lowered its head and sniffed at Luc. A long tongue rolled from its jaws and licked Luc over the side of his face. The rough surface stripped away layers of skin like sandpaper.

Luc roared in pain as the creature dug its claws deeper. Matt had gotten to his feet. He took aim and squeezed the trigger several times. The bullets hit the mass of black fur, and clearly penetrated the skin beneath, for the small streaks of blood stood out against its coat.

"Run to the Spider," Luc called out with his final breath. The large cat jerked its powerful forelegs and ripped Luc in half from his crown down to his groin. Blood erupted from the body in a wave, and the beast lapped at the spurts like it was a water fountain.

Matt found power in his legs and broke into a run. He could see the red glow from the Spider, and with the beast distracted, he knew that he had every chance of making his escape.

Matt ran, his feet slipped and skidded on the slick rock, but somehow he managed to stay his course. Behind him the creature had finished chewing on Luc and had given chase. Its heavy strides gained ground on Matt with each moment.

The Spider was ahead, but as Matt grew closer, he realized that the power orb was shrinking. Somebody was powering the machine down. Finding the extra impetus that he needed, Matt pushed harder. He flung himself through the air, hoping to make it through the portal before it closed. Pain exploded in his leg, however, and he was pulled back down to earth. The cat-beast had struck out at the right moment, and its claws had torn through the skin and muscle of Matt's leg, splitting his thigh in two. Matt screamed from the pain, and roared in anger. He had come too far to die.

The cat-beast stood over him, its face was soaked with blood, and strips of Luc's flesh hung from its whiskers.

The cat opened its mouth, revealing the large incisors that would tear a man apart in seconds.

The dinosaur came out of nowhere, bounding over the rocks. Matt had no time to dwell on the sight, for it was over in a second. The cat was gone, shunted over the edge of the volcano, and the dinosaur went with it. The creature with a large domed head had rammed the cat-beast from the side. Stunning it. As the two fell, the dinosaur resumed its attack, launching strike after strike with its head, crushing the body and head of the beast.

Matt looked up, craning his head back to see behind him. He almost choked on the rain, but he saw the Spider. The orb was fading fast, but he could still make it.

His leg was bleeding, pumping blood onto the ground with every heartbeat. Matt grew weaker by the second, but somehow he managed to pull himself onto the Spider platform and he was safe. The red light enveloped him and Matt looked up at the world he had been in. He saw a large group of pteranodons flying high above him, their shadows black against the stormy sky. Then everything was gone. Dissolved into a haze of red.

That was when he heard the gunshot.

CHAPTER 16

Julian lay on the floor. He should be dead. The third shot should have killed him. He opened his eyes. Pain was all he knew. His body was a ball of agony. His hands, which he held clamped against his stomach, were slick with blood. It filled his mouth, and made his head swim.

Julian forced himself to raise his head. The Spider was dying. The timer he had set had come into effect. The sensors were being overloaded with a steadily increasing charge. Julian was the only one who knew how to replace them, and repair the damage that would be done to the machine itself. He had seen to that in its design.

Albert was in front of the Spider. He was not standing anymore, but had collapsed to his knees. A bloody mass of flesh and bone shards was where his left eye should have been. Blood dribbled from his mouth as he tried to talk and raise his now gunless hand. He failed, and fell forward, landing on his face, crushing his nose with a wet smack as he struck the cold floor.

Behind him, slumped over the steps of the Spider was the young doctor Julian had sent through into the other world.

"I'm sorry," Julian whispered as he stared at the man.

Blood poured down the steps of the Spider, and Julian could see the mangled lump of flesh that had been Matt's leg. It had ripped further from his body in the final moments of his scramble, and now held on only by a single strand of flesh that refused to quit.

"Don't be." Matt smiled, and laid his head down to rest. The gun fell from his hands and clattered to the floor. Matt closed his eyes and saw the best moments of his life play out. A life he had dedicated to others at the sacrifice of anything for himself. He had no regrets, no last wishes, or unfinished business. So when death came and laid claim to his soul, Matt offered no resistance. He slid into the cold embrace of forever and was finally at peace.

Julian turned his body, grunting as pain exploded from his gut. He knew how bad it was. He knew that he too was dying. The lab he had helped to found had become nothing more than a mausoleum. Turning, ignoring the pain, he looked at Tracy.

He reached out a trembling arm, hoping to hold her one last time, but someone moved in the way. A man in an expensive suit smiled down at Julian.

"My my, Dr. Grau. This is an unfortunate predicament. You see, Albert was always a loose cannon. His death will create new opportunities, but there are plenty of eager people ready to move up the ranks. As you can understand, our organization always has a back-up plan, and people ready to step up to the challenge," the stranger spoke. "The question is what to do with you," the man sneered, and his face had the same cold, reptilian look.

Julian opened his mouth to speak, but all he could do was cough up a lungful of blood.

"Help me," he managed, wheezing the words over his lips.

"With pleasure, Dr. Grau, but you must understand. The very best medical care does not come cheap. If you wish to live, then you must give us something in return." The man, who spoke with a heavy accent, stared at Julian, unmoved by the scene unfolding before him.

Julian was unable to speak. He opened his mouth and gasped several times, that was the best he could do.

"I understand. It can be hard to speak. Your time really is running out, so listen very carefully. Blink once for yes and twice for no. Will you repair and run the Spider for us? In return, you will live, you will be a key man in our family, and that in itself comes with its own rewards." The man smiled, and Julian thought he could see the face of the devil hiding behind the human features.

Staring at the man, Julian held firm. He hoped that as his life slipped away, the pain he felt would lessen. If anything, it got worse the closer he came to the end.

Julian closed his eyes. He wanted death to come for him, but it wouldn't. The angel of mercy was not there to collect his soul. Once he was sure that Tracy was free, truly free from the prison, Julian opened his eyes and held the gaze that met him.

"A very wise choice, Dr. Grau, a very wise choice indeed."

THE END

CHECK OUT OTHER GREAT
DINOSAUR THRILLERS

THE VALLEY
by Rick Jones

In a dystopian future, a self-contained valley in Argentina serves as the 'far arena' for those convicted of a crime. Inside the Valley: carnivorous dinosaurs generated from preserved DNA. The goal: cross the Valley to get to the Gates of Freedom. The chance of survival: no one has ever completed the journey. Convicted of crimes with little or no merit, Ben Peyton and others must battle their way across fields filled with the world's deadliest apex predators in order to reach salvation. All the while the journey is caught on cameras and broadcast to the world as a reality show, the deaths and killings real, the macabre appetite of the audience needing to be satiated as Ben Peyton leads his team to escape not only from a legal system that's more interested in entertainment than in justice, but also from the predators of the Valley.

JURASSIC DEAD
by Rick Chesler & David Sakmyster

An Antarctic research team hoping to study microbial organisms in an underground lake discovers something far more amazing: perfectly preserved dinosaur corpses. After one thaws and wakes ravenously hungry, it becomes apparent that death, like life, will find a way.
Environmental activist Alex Ramirez, son of the expedition's paleontologist, came to Antarctica to defend the organisms from extinction, but soon learns that it is the human race that needs protecting.

CHECK OUT OTHER GREAT
DINOSAUR THRILLERS

LOST WORLD OF PATAGONIA
by Dane Hatchell

An earthquake opens a path to a land hidden for millions of years. Under the guise of finding cryptid animals, Ace Corporation sends Alex Klasse, a Cryptozoologist and university professor, his associates, and a band of mercenaries to explore the Lost World of Patagonia. The crew boards a nuclear powered All-Terrain Tracked Carrier and takes a harrowing ride into the unknown.

The expedition soon discovers prehistoric creatures still exist. But the dangers won't prevent a sub-team from leaving the group in search of rare jewels. Tensions run high as personalities clash, and man proves to be just as deadly as the dinosaurs that roam the countryside.

Lost World of Patagonia is a prehistoric thriller filled with murder, mayhem, and savage dinosaur action.

SAVAGE ISLAND
by Alan Spencer

Somewhere in the Atlantic Ocean, an uncharted island has been used for the illegal dumping of chemicals and pollutants for years by Globo Corp's. Private investigator Pierce Range will learn plenty about the evil conglomerate when Susan Branch, an environmentalist from The Green Project, hires him to join the expedition to save her kidnapped father from Globo Corp's evil hands.

Things go to hell in a hurry once the team reaches the island. The bloodthirsty dinosaurs and voracious cannibals are only the beginning of the fight for survival. Pierce must unlock the mysteries surrounding the toxic operation and somehow remain in one piece to complete the rescue mission.

Ratchet up the body count, because this mission will leave the killing floor soaked in blood and chewed up corpses. When the insane battle ends, will there by anybody left alive to survive Savage Island?